I Can Read Comics introduces children to the world of graphic novel storytelling and encourages visual literacy in emerging readers. Comics inspire reader engagement unlike any other format. They ask readers to infer and answer questions, like:

1. What do I read first? Image or text?
2. Why is this word balloon shaped this way, and that word balloon shaped that way?
3. Why is a character making that facial expression? Are they happy, angry, excited, sad?

From the comics your child reads with you to the first comic they read on their own, there are **I Can Read Comics** for every stage of reading:

LEVEL 1

Simple stories for shared reading.

LEVEL 2

Engaging stories for children reading on their own.

LEVEL 3

Complex stories for independent readers.

The magic of graphic novel storytelling lies between the gutters.
Unlock the magic with...

I Can Read Comics!

Visit **ICanRead.com** for information on enriching your child's reading experience.

I Can Read *Comics* Cartooning Basics

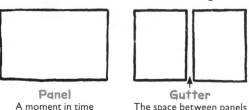

Panel
A moment in time

Gutter
The space between panels

Tier
One row of panels

Word Balloons — When someone talks, thinks, whispers, or screams, their words go in here:

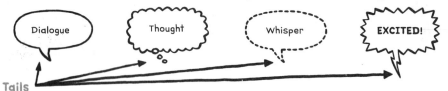

Dialogue

Thought

Whisper

EXCITED!

Tails
Point to whoever is talking / thinking / whispering / screaming / etc.

A quick how-to-read comics guide:

In a **panel**, read the text on the **left** first.

Then, read the text on the **right**.

On a page, **start here**, in the **top left** corner!

After that, read the panel immediately to the **right**.

When you're done up there, come down here and read **this** panel **next**!

ME NEXT! ME NEXT!

You're almost there...

YAY!

YOU MADE IT! You just read a comic page!

Remember to...
Read the text along with the image, paying close attention to the character's acting, the action, and/or the scene. Every little detail matters!

No dialogue? No problem!
If there is no dialogue within a panel, take the time to read the image. Visual cues are just as important as text, so don't forget about them!

HarperAlley is an imprint of HarperCollins Publishers.
I Can Read® and I Can Read Book® are trademarks of HarperCollins Publishers.

My Little Pony: Sunny's Day
MY LITTLE PONY and all related characters are trademarks of Hasbro and are used with permission.
© 2022 Hasbro. All Rights Reserved. Licensed by Hasbro.

Library of Congress Control Number: 2021944120
ISBN 978-0-06-303748-9

Book design by Elaine Lopez-Levine
21 22 23 24 25 LSCC 10 9 8 7 6 5 4 3 2 1 ❖ First Edition

I Can Read! Comics
LEVEL 1

MY LITTLE PONY

WITHDRAWN

SUNNY'S DAY

MEGAN ROTH   AGNES GARBOWSKA

HARPER alley

An Imprint of HarperCollinsPublishers

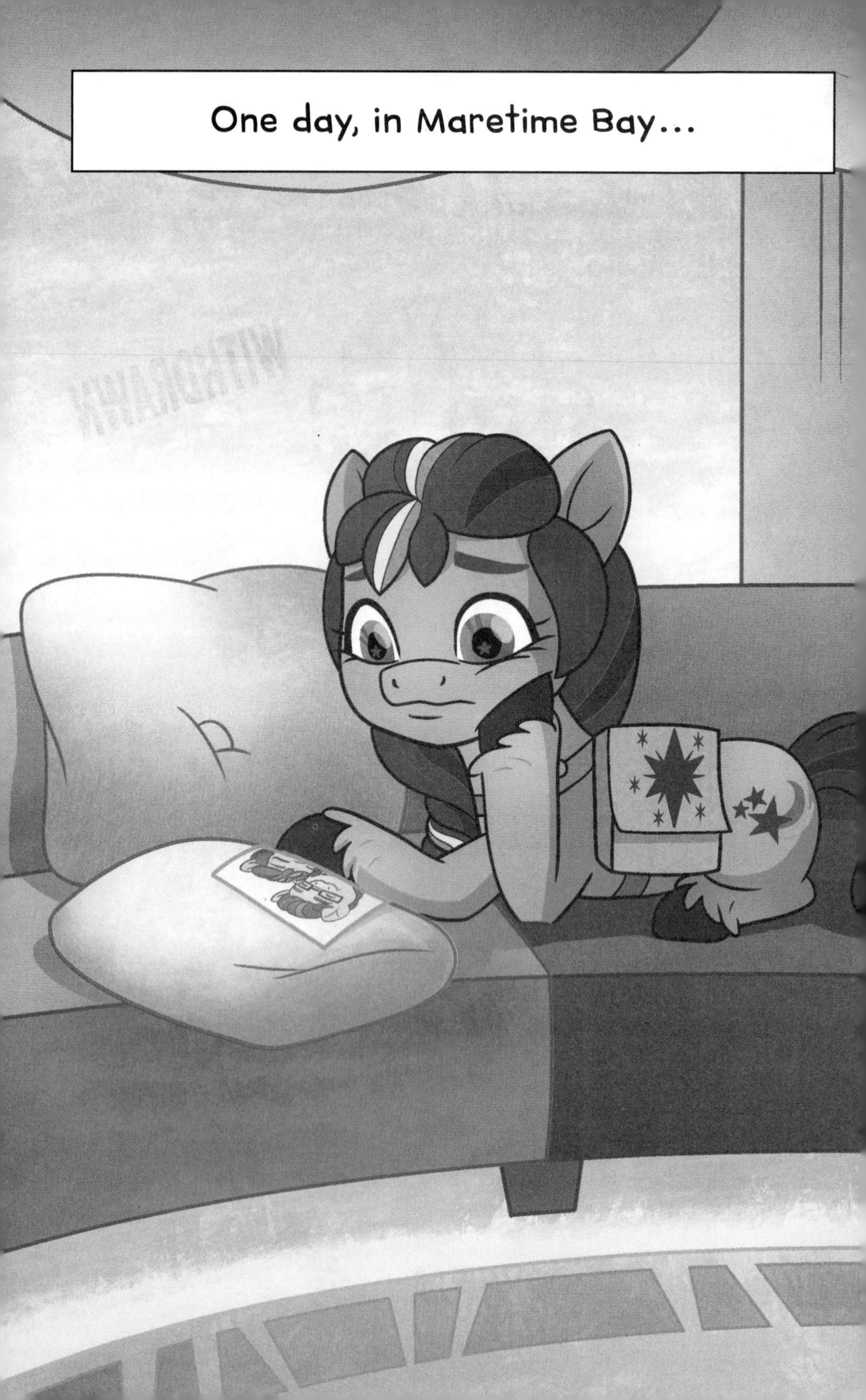
One day, in Maretime Bay...

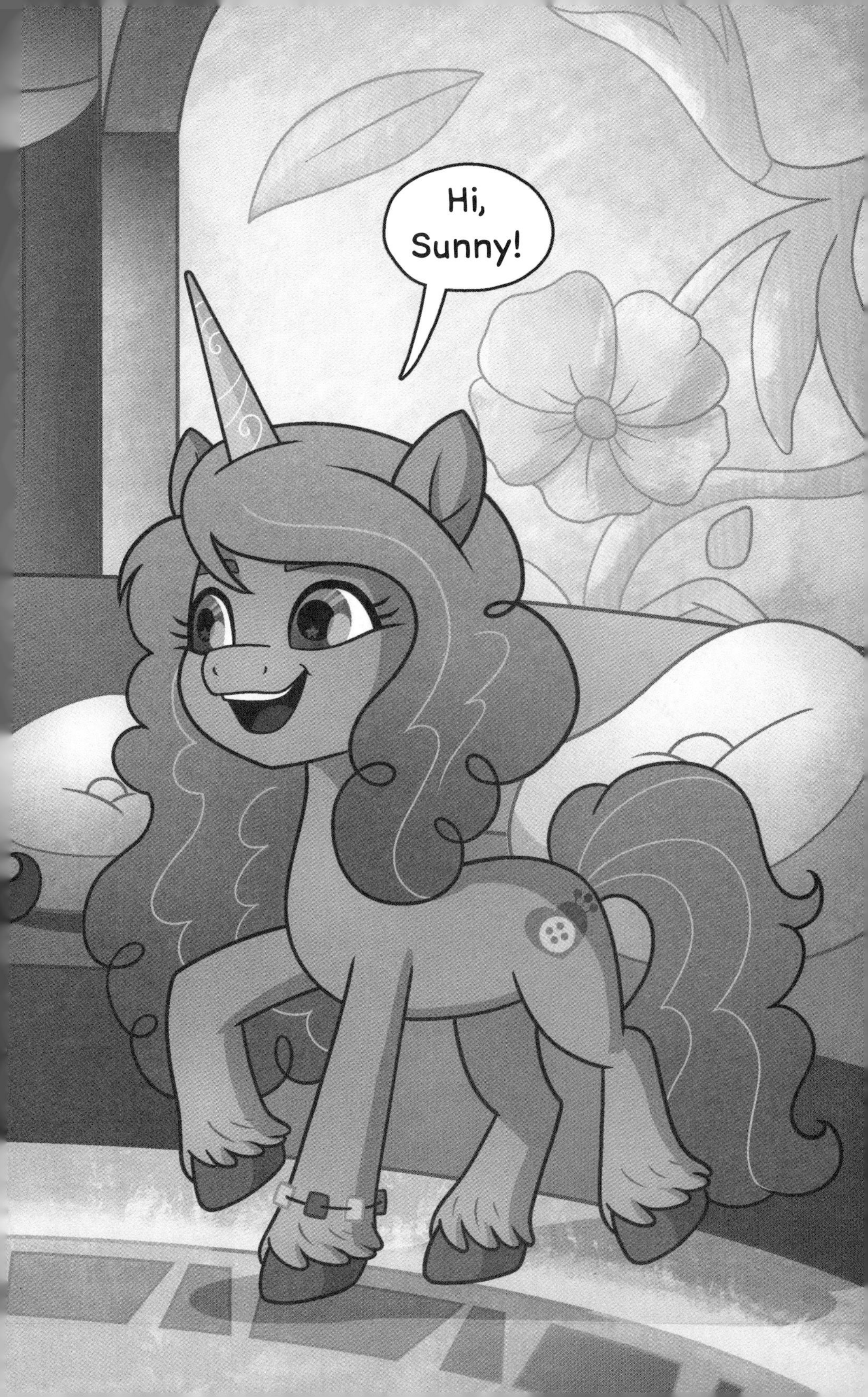
Hi,
Sunny!

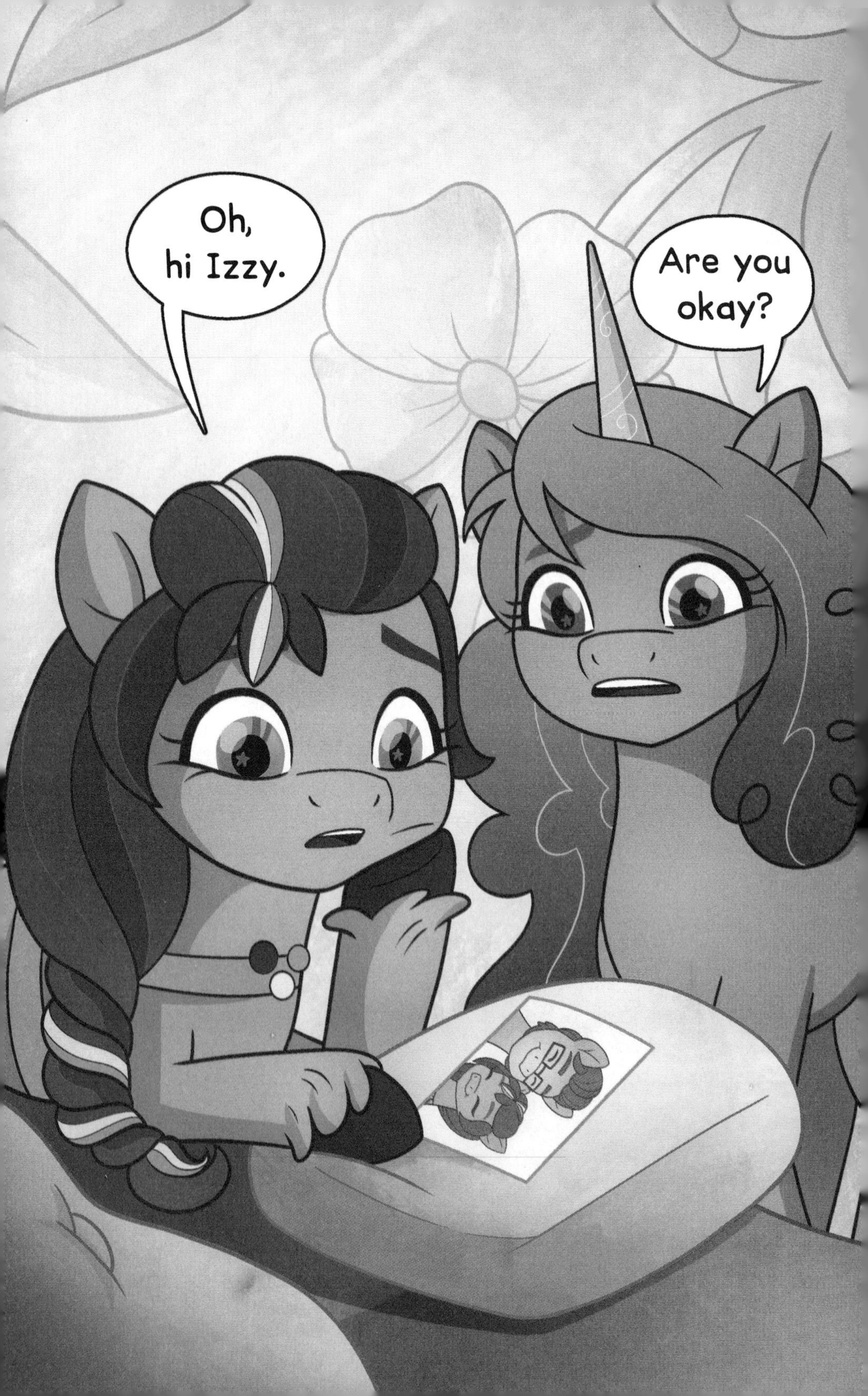
Oh, hi Izzy.
Are you okay?

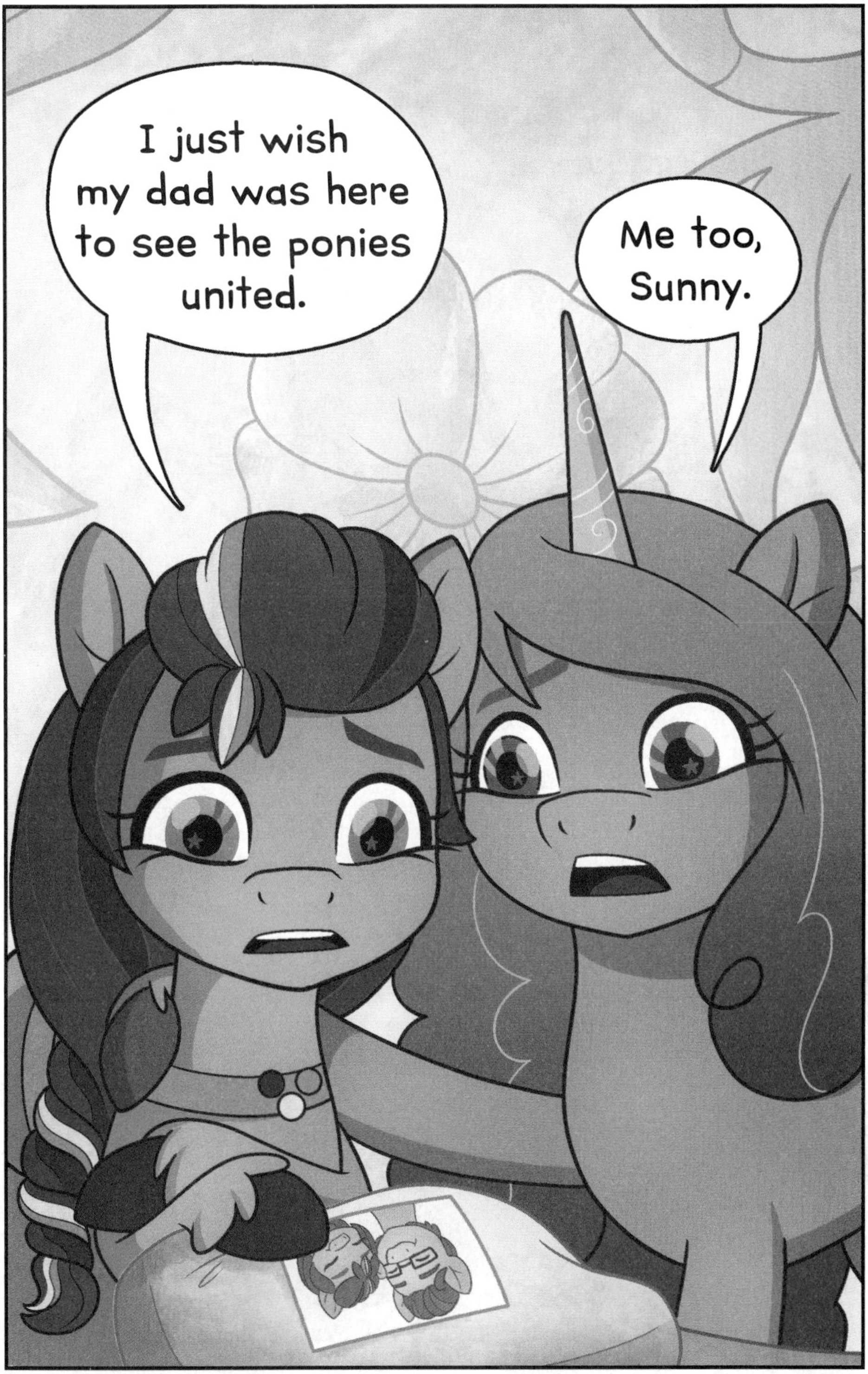
I just wish my dad was here to see the ponies united.
Me too, Sunny.

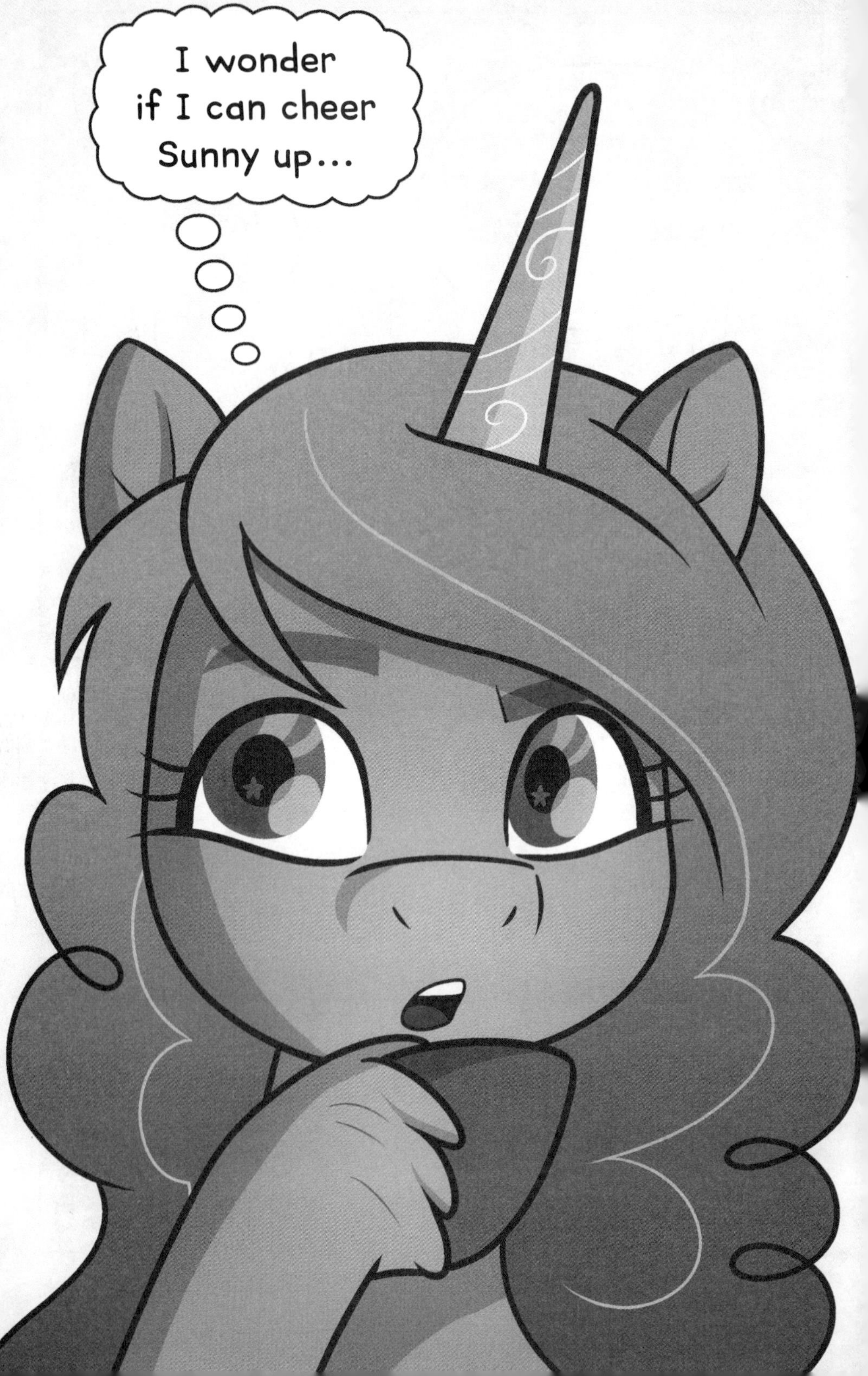
I wonder if I can cheer Sunny up...

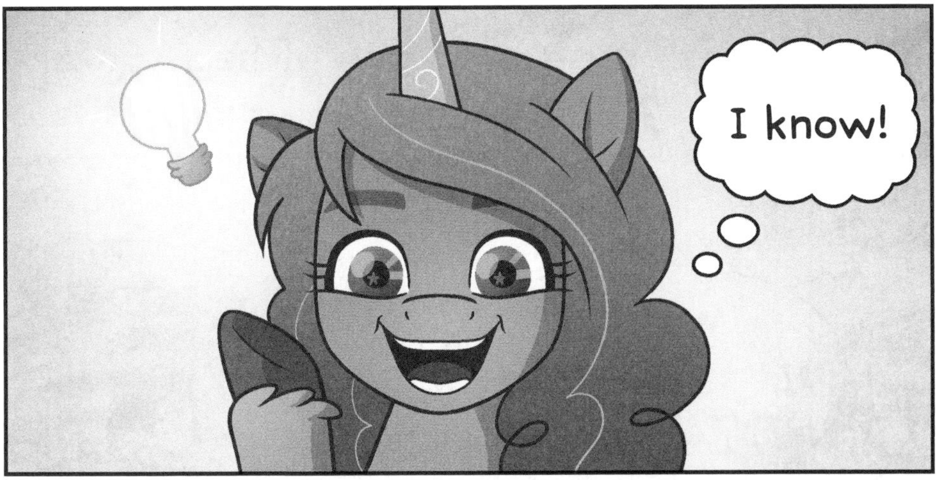
I know!

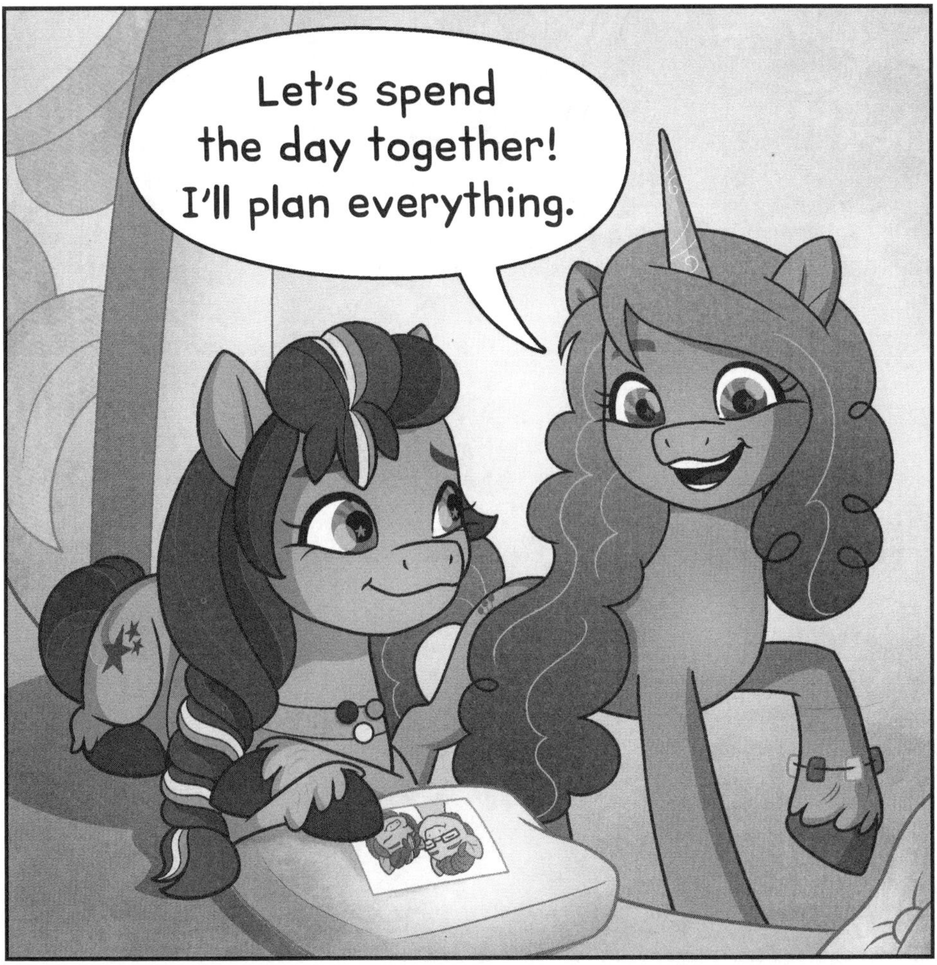
Let's spend the day together! I'll plan everything.

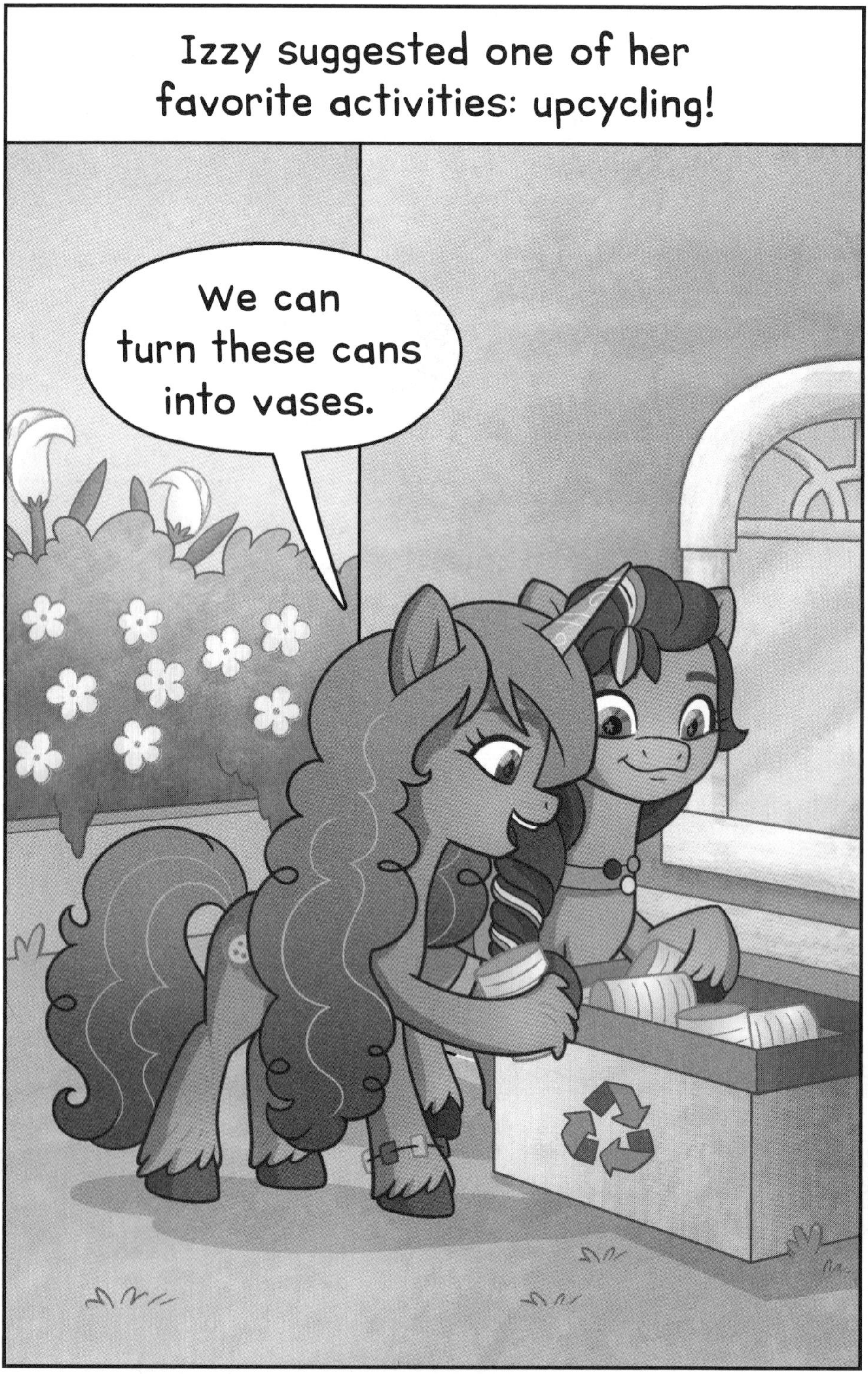
Izzy suggested one of her favorite activities: upcycling!
We can turn these cans into vases.

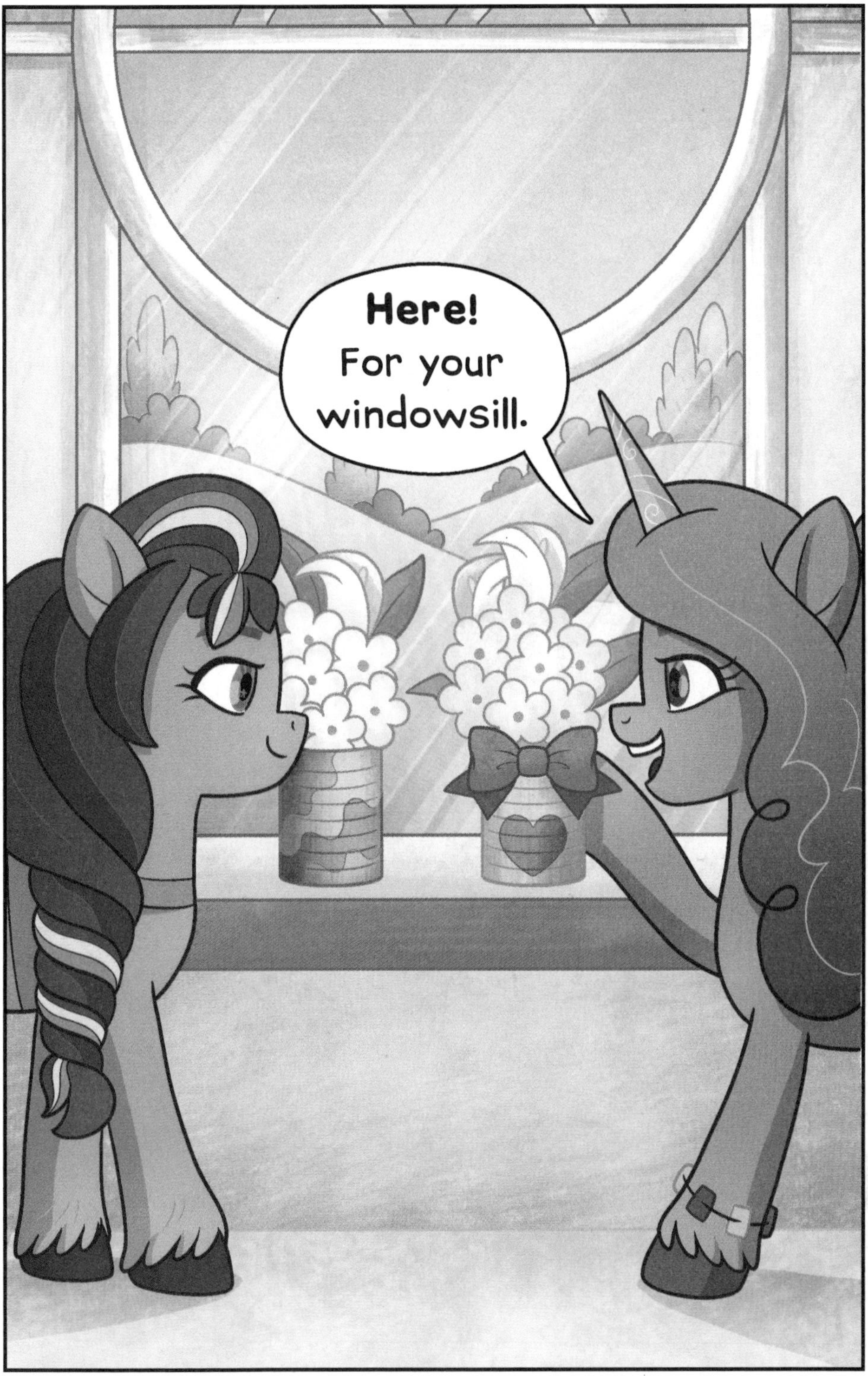
Here! For your windowsill.

Next, Izzy suggested a new game:
a tea party!

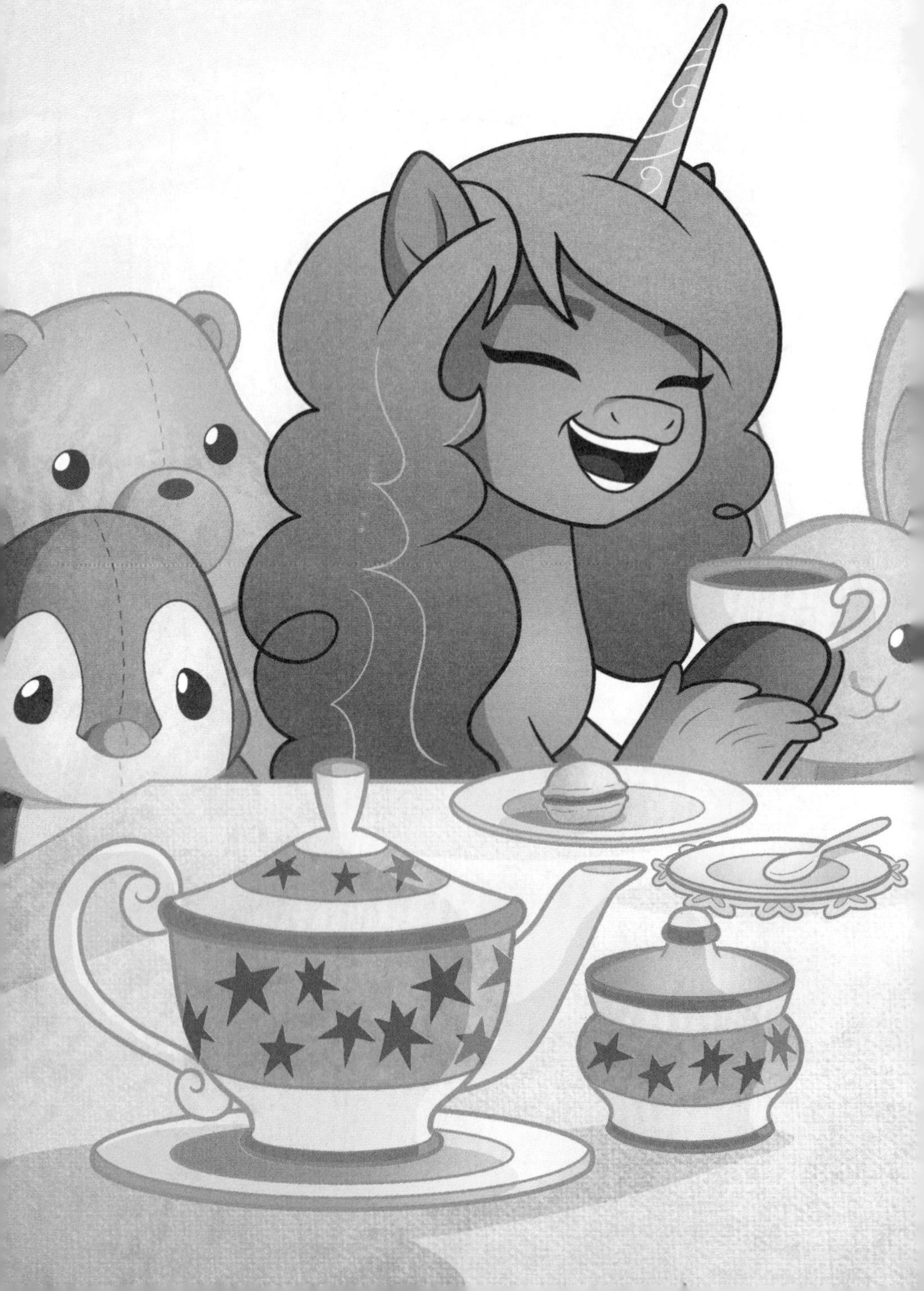

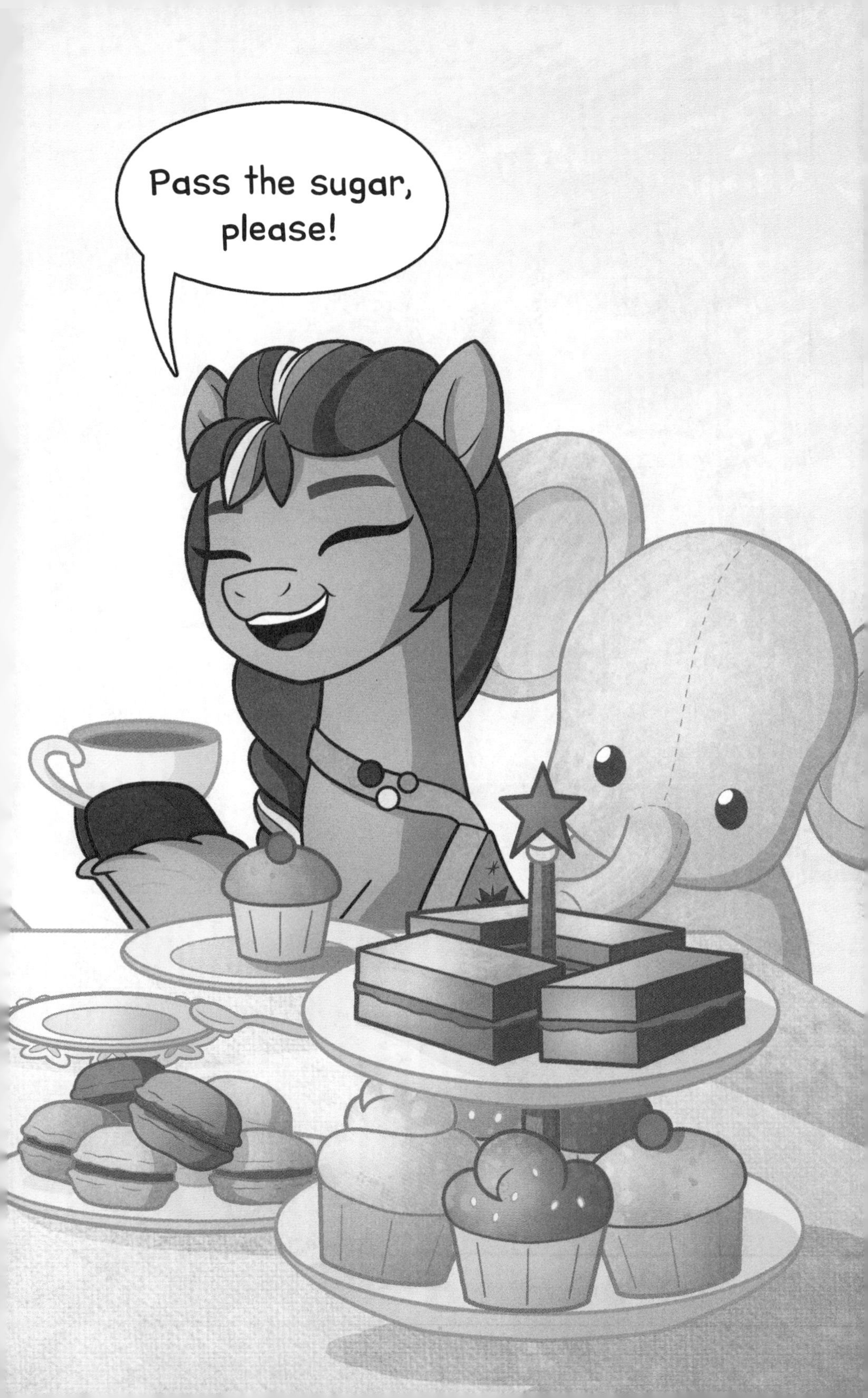
Pass the sugar, please!

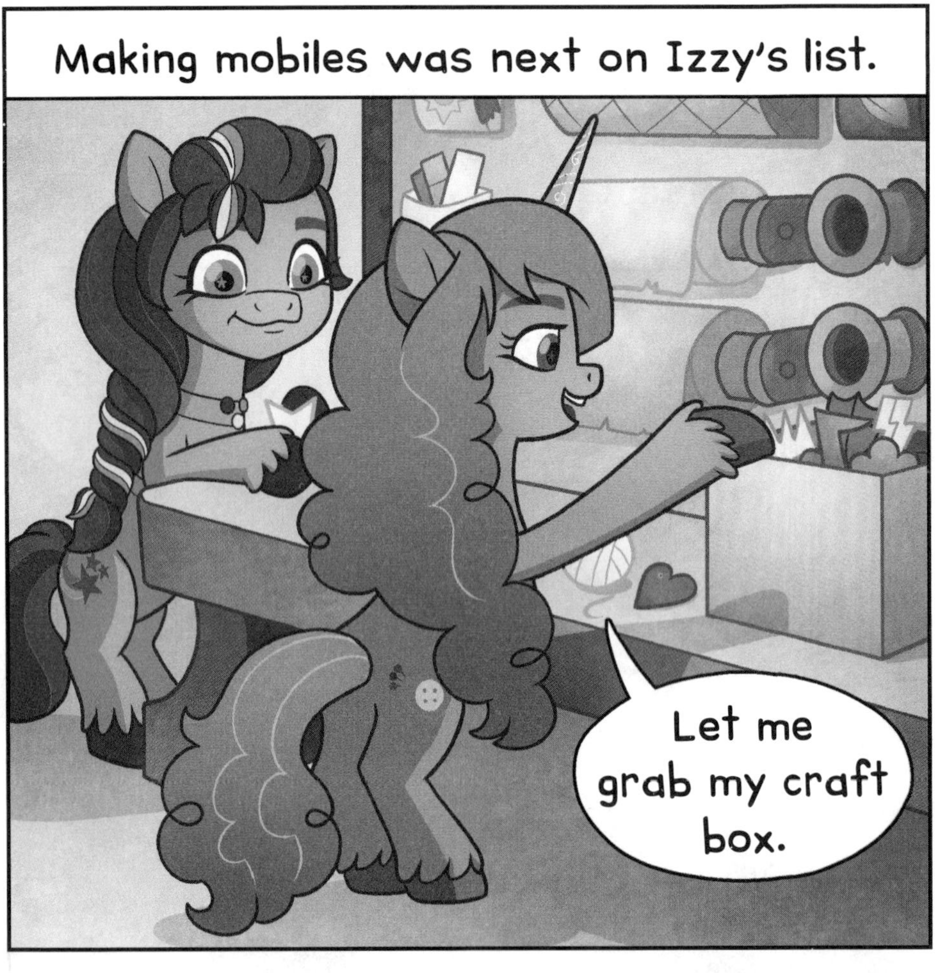
Making mobiles was next on Izzy's list.
Let me grab my craft box.
Almost done...

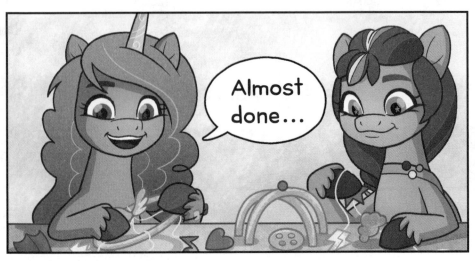

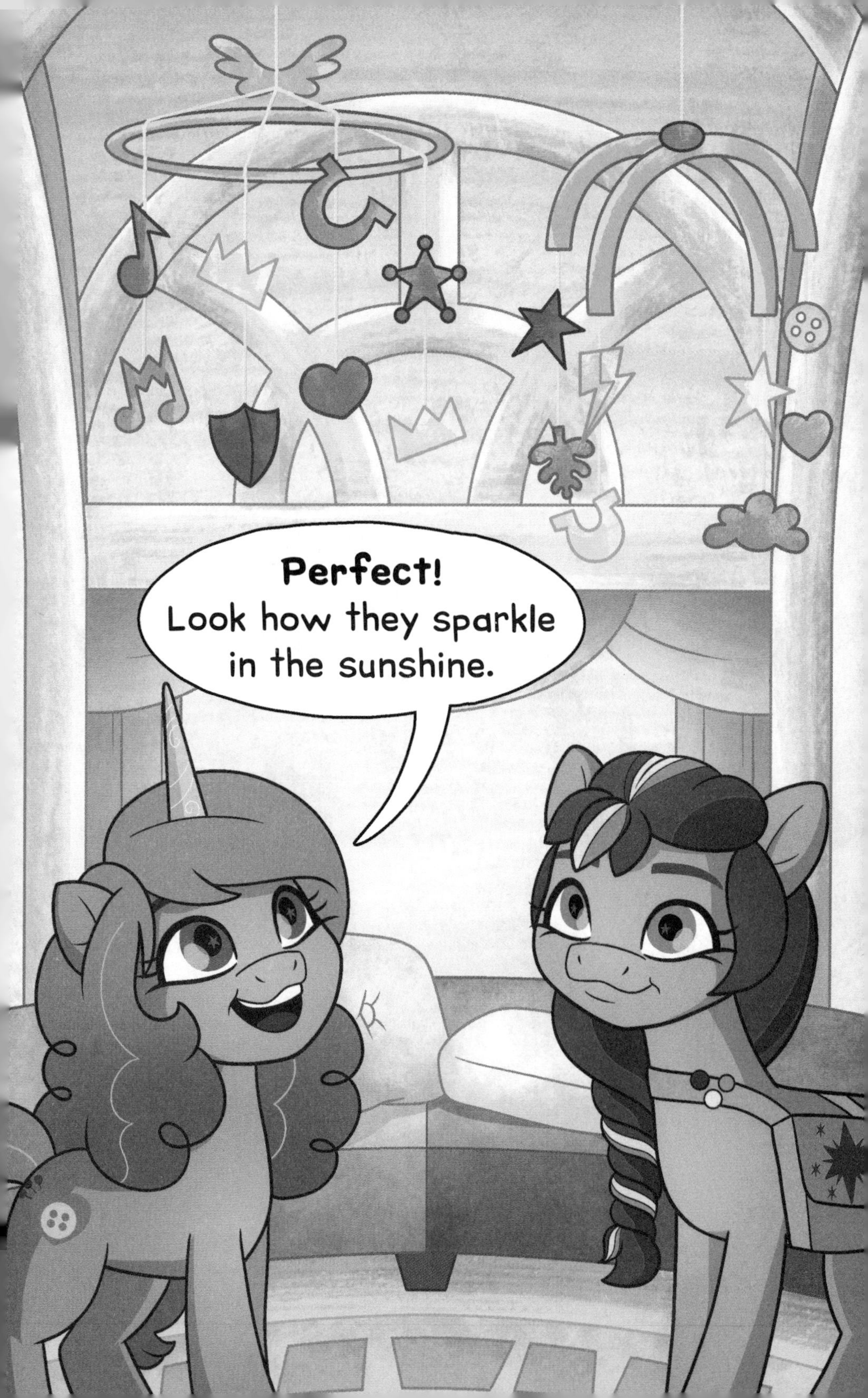
Perfect!
Look how they sparkle in the sunshine.

Izzy and Sunny painted a picture of the Mane 5.

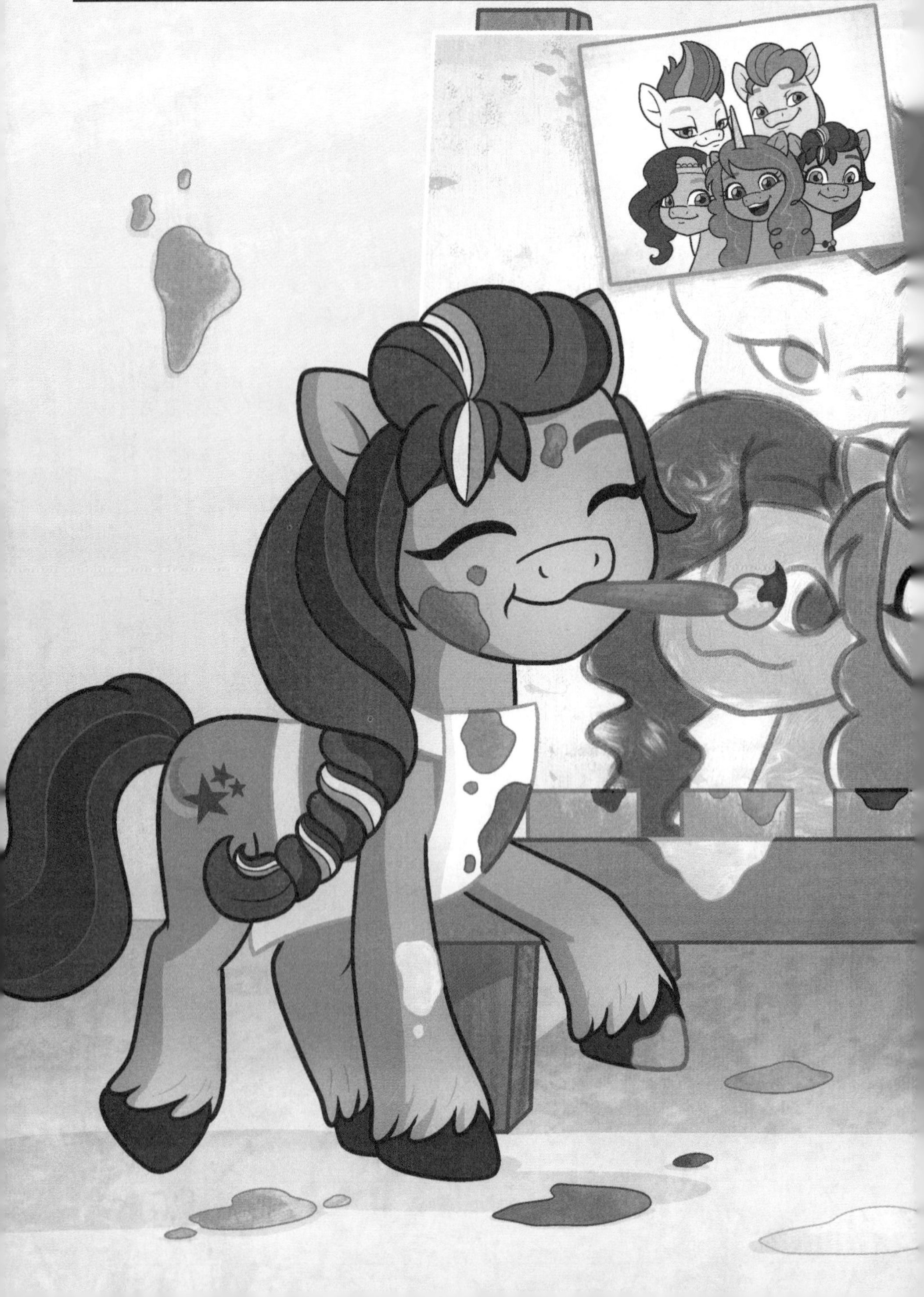

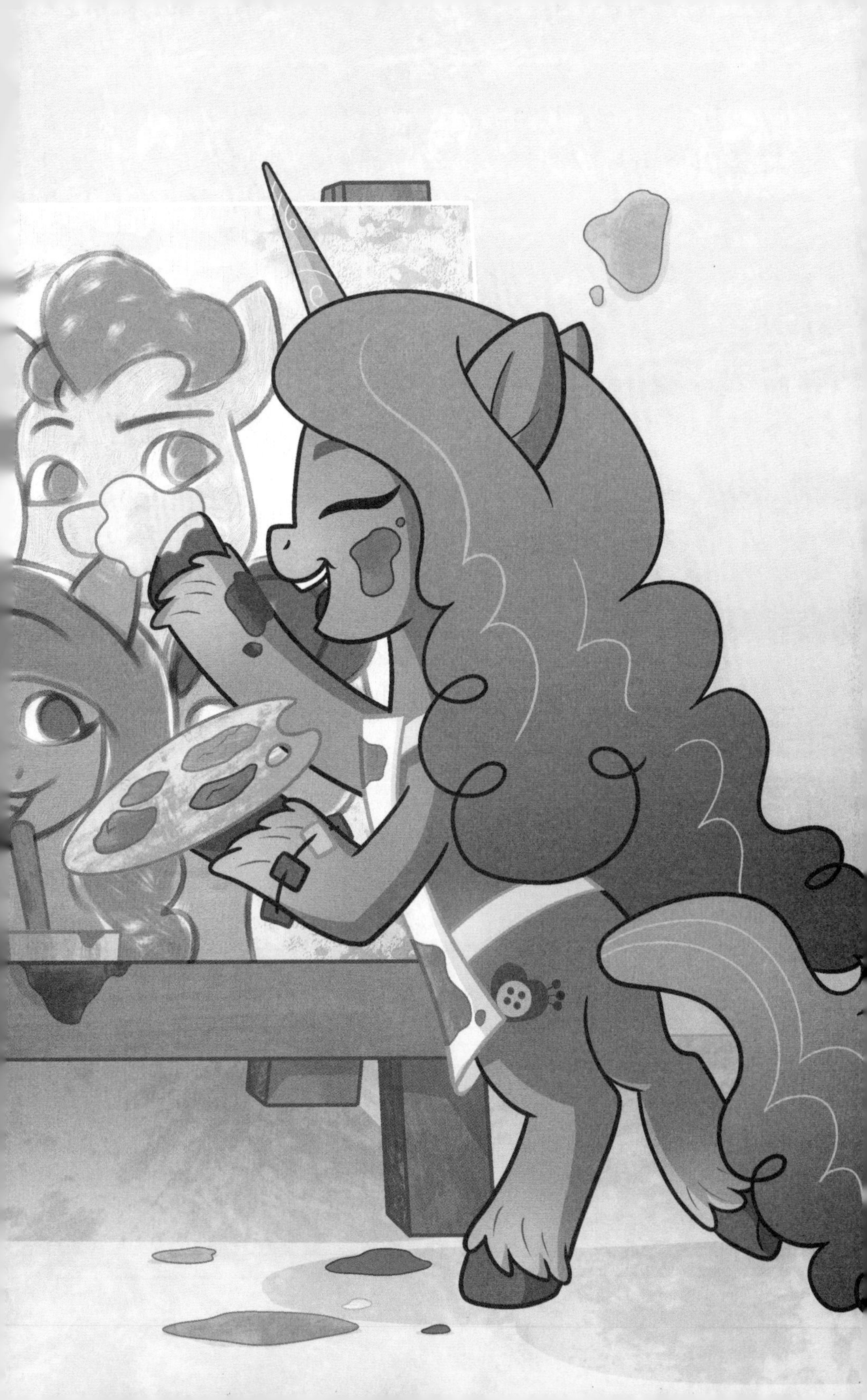

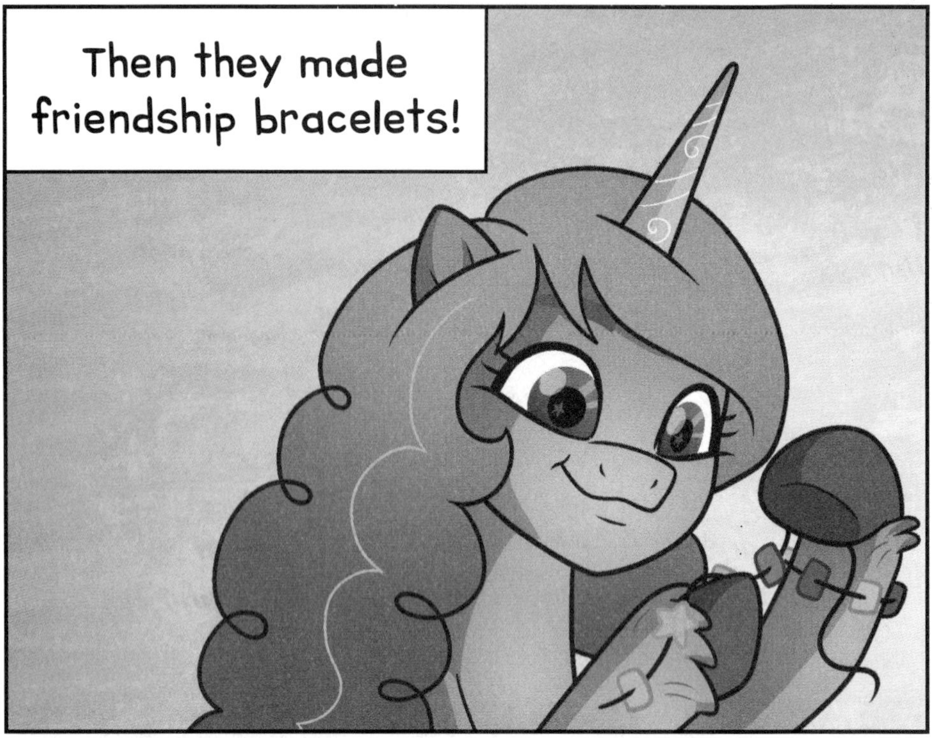
Then they made friendship bracelets!

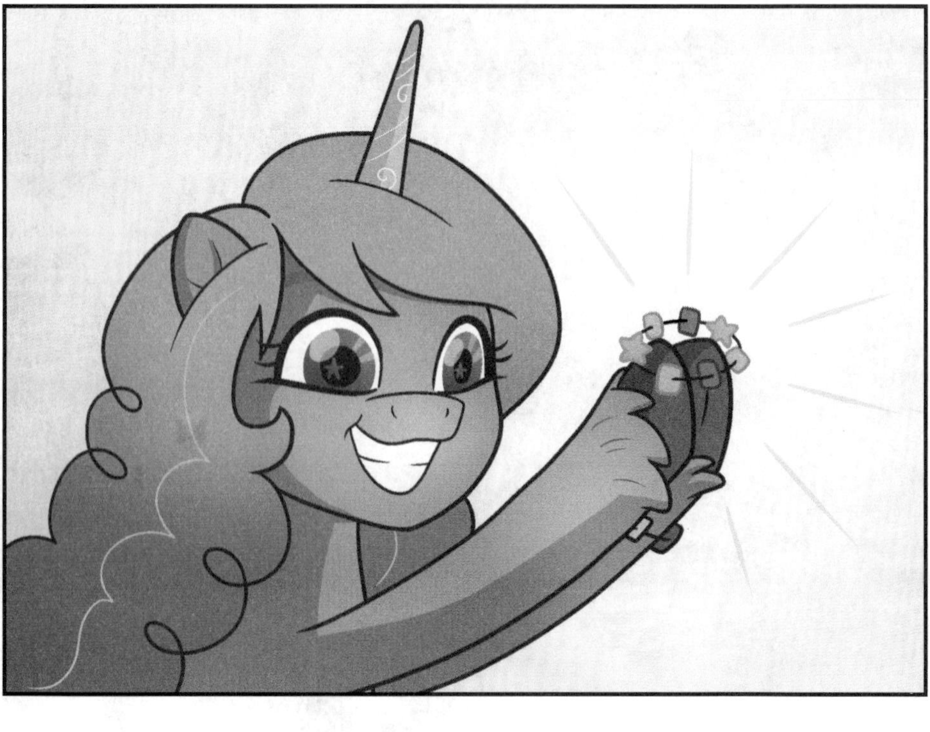

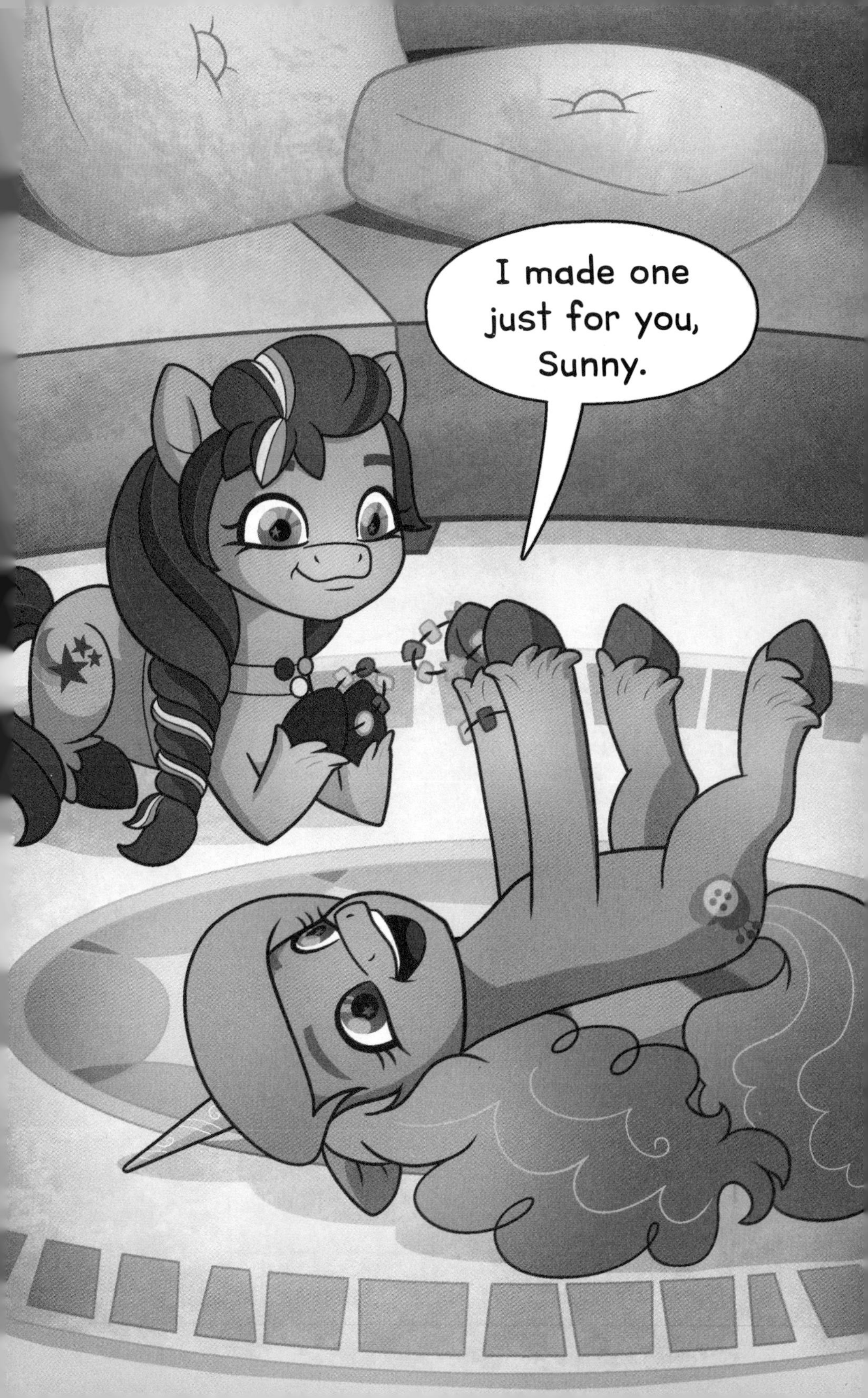
I made one just for you, Sunny.

Next they made their own instruments.

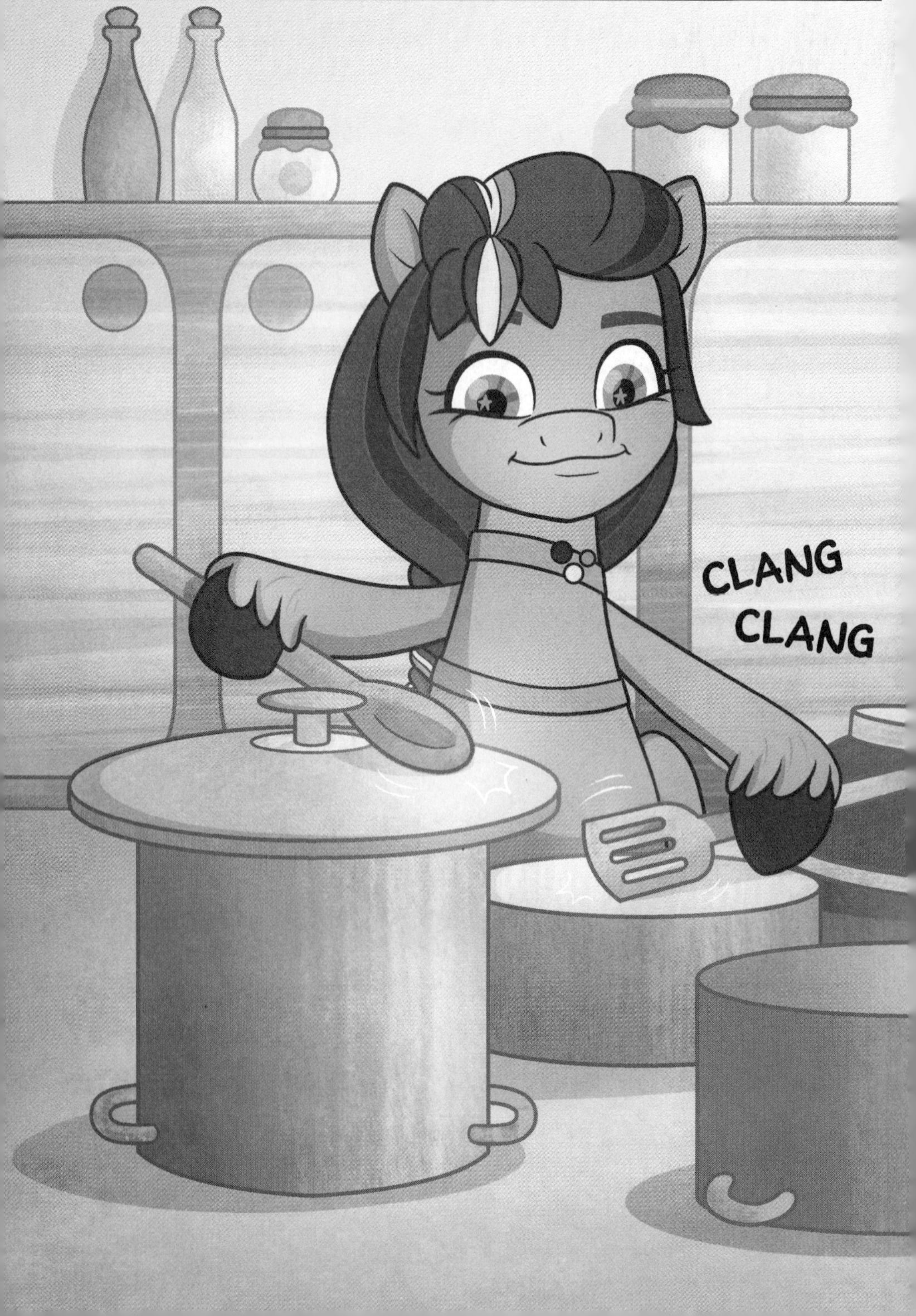
CLANG
CLANG

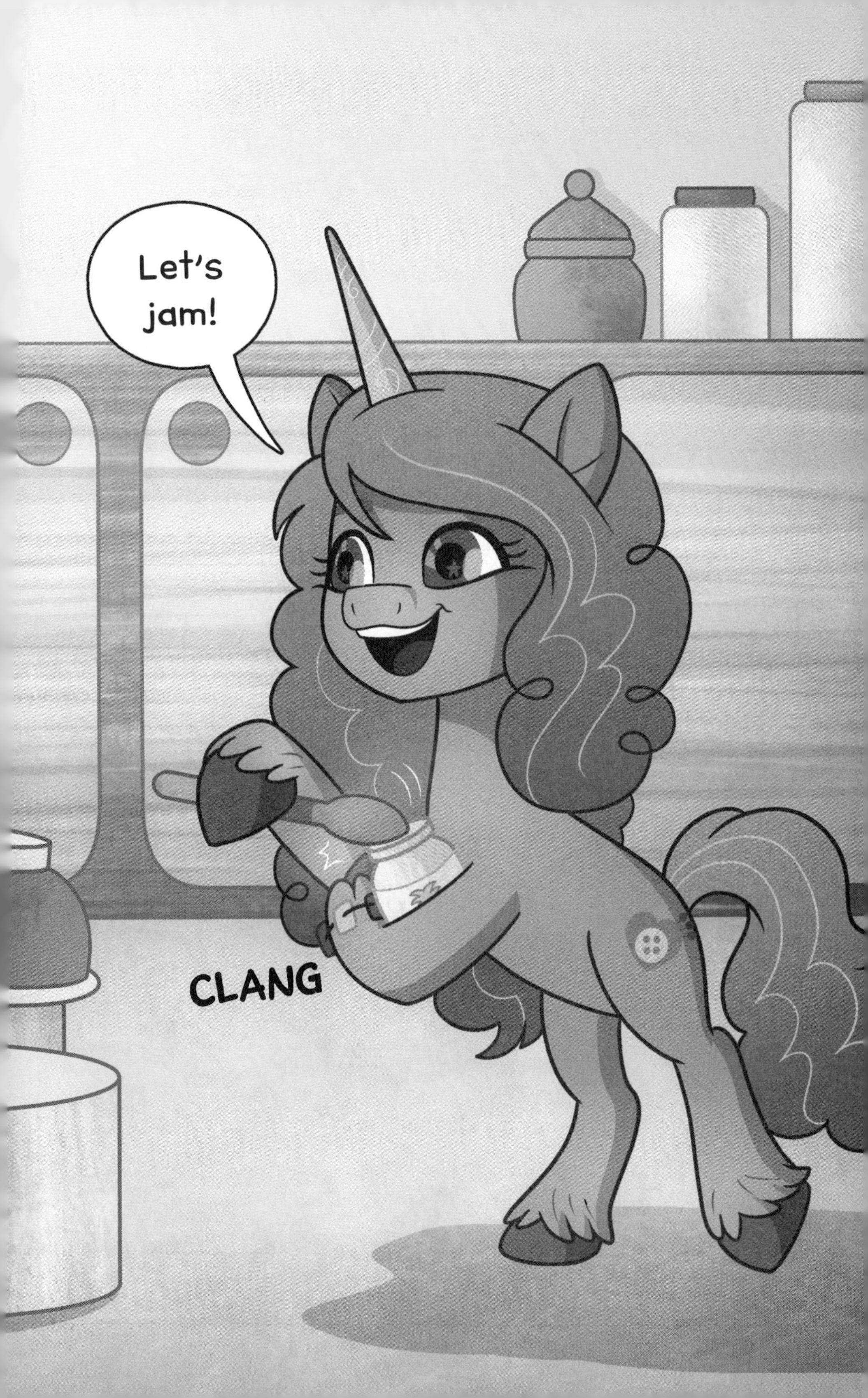
Let's jam!
CLANG

But then Izzy noticed
Sunny **still** looked sad.

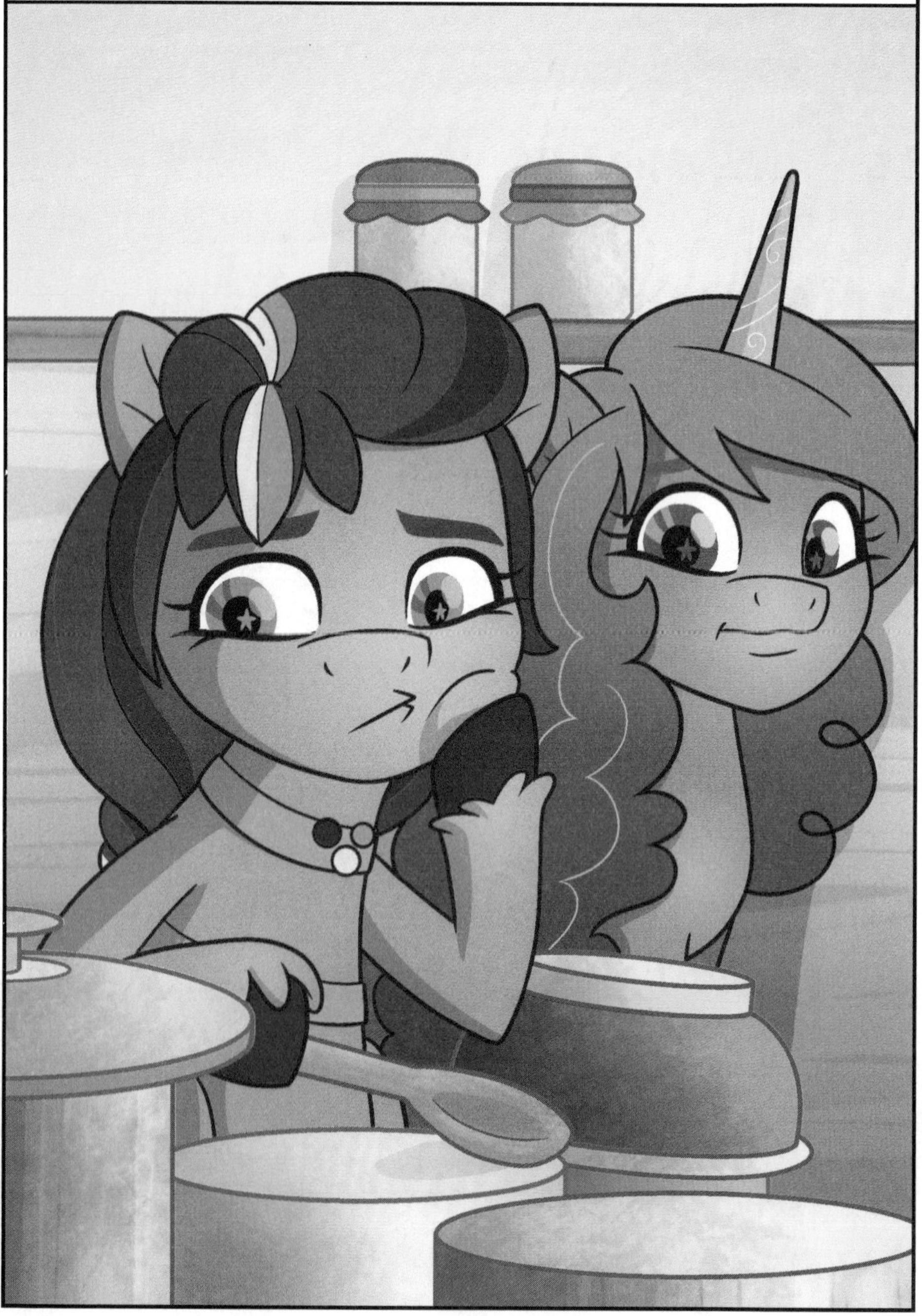

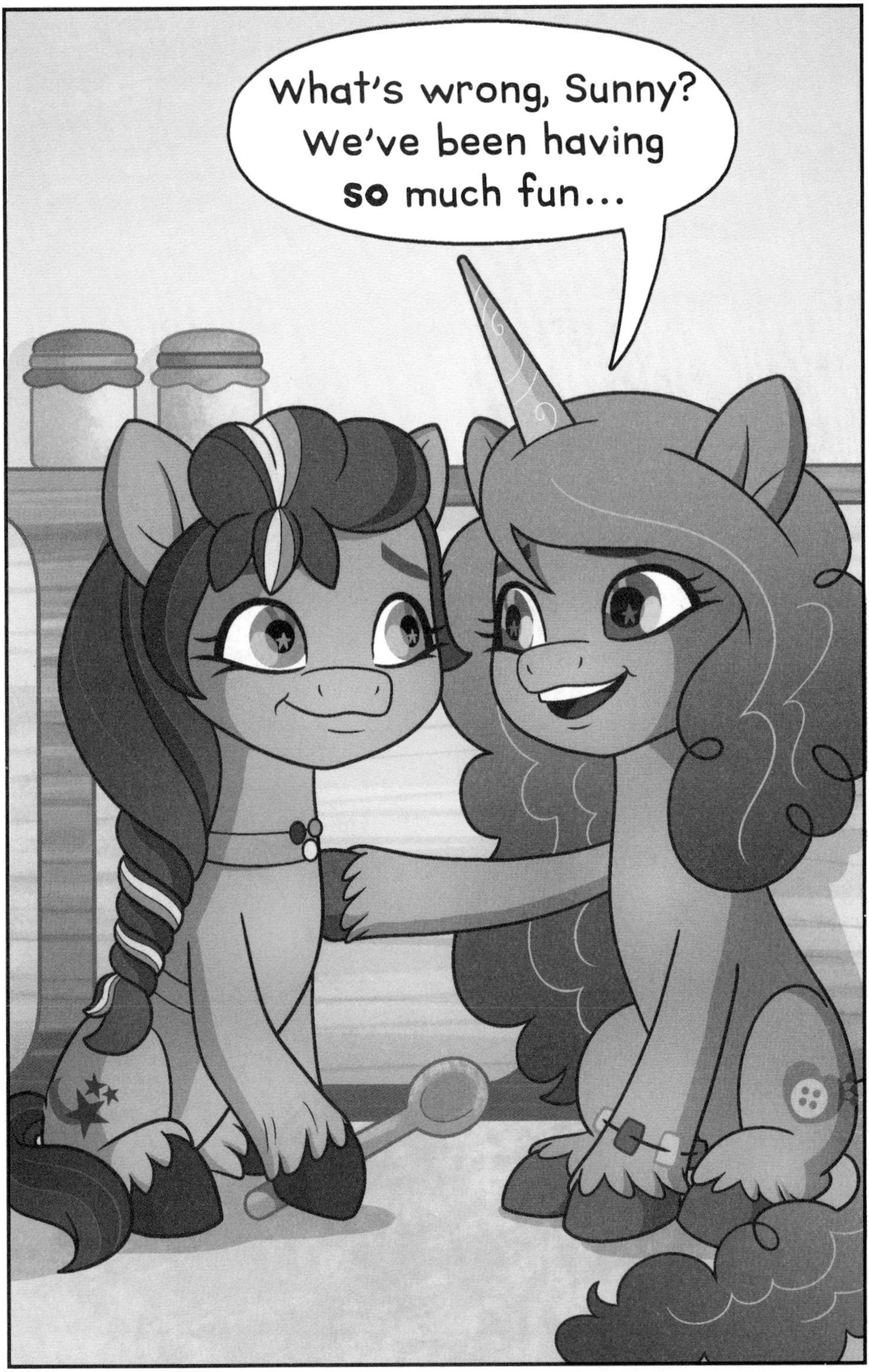
What's wrong, Sunny? We've been having **so** much fun...

...We upcycled, had a tea party, and made mobiles...

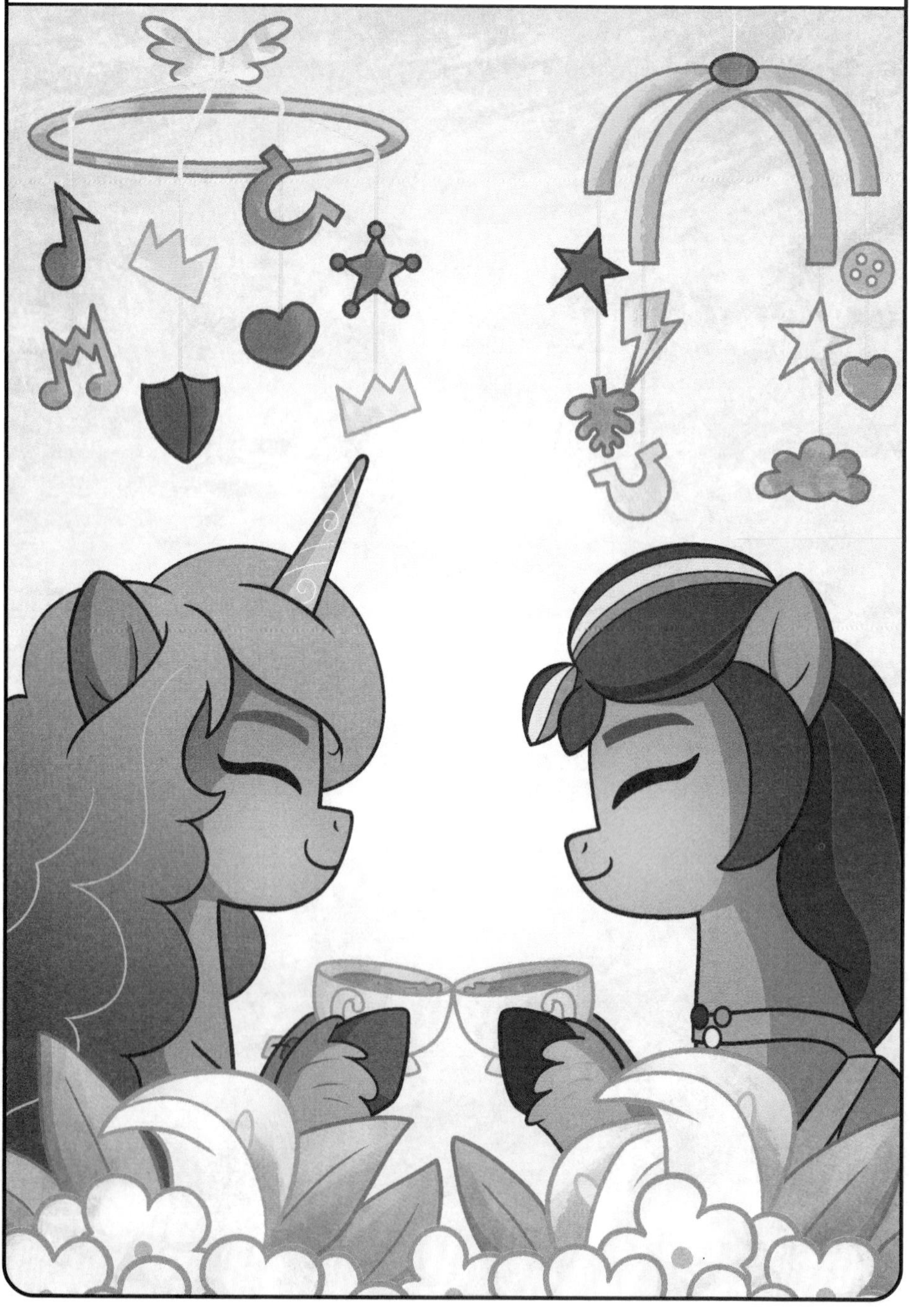

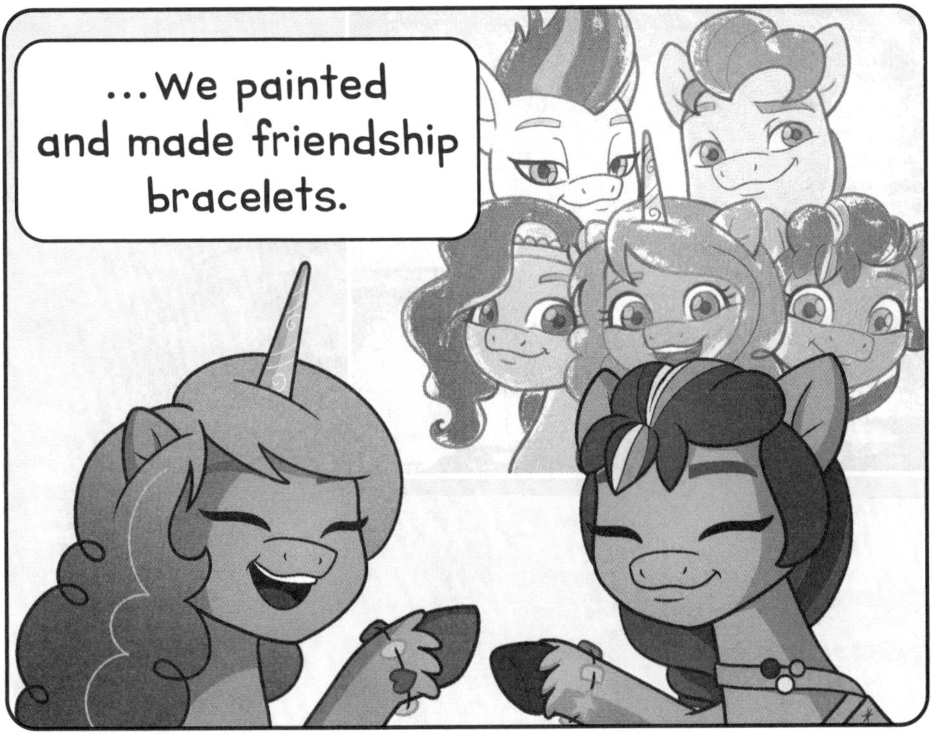
...We painted and made friendship bracelets.

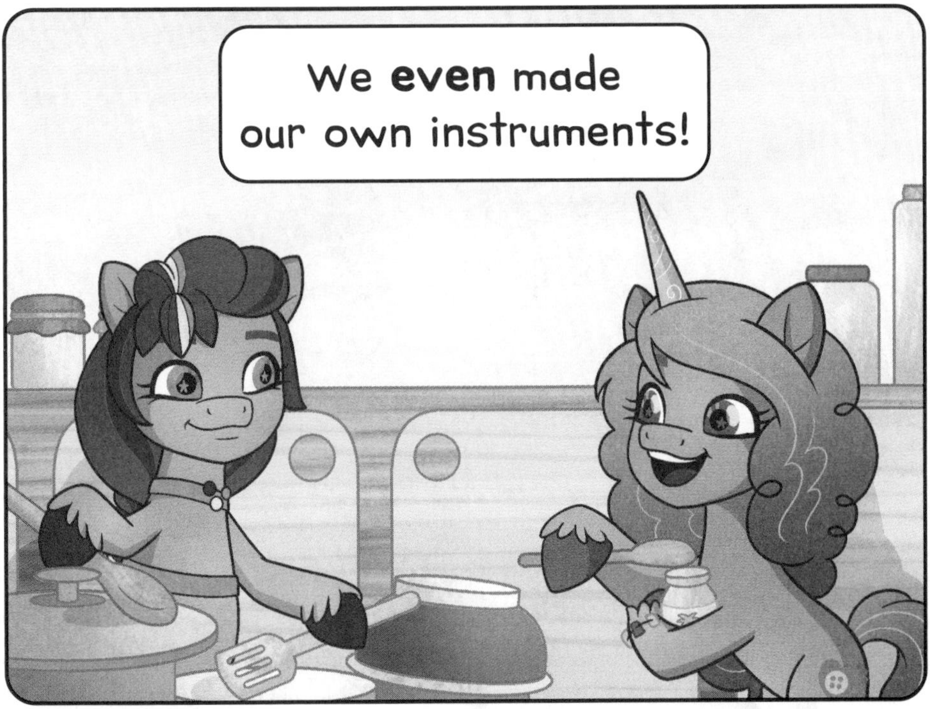
We **even** made our own instruments!

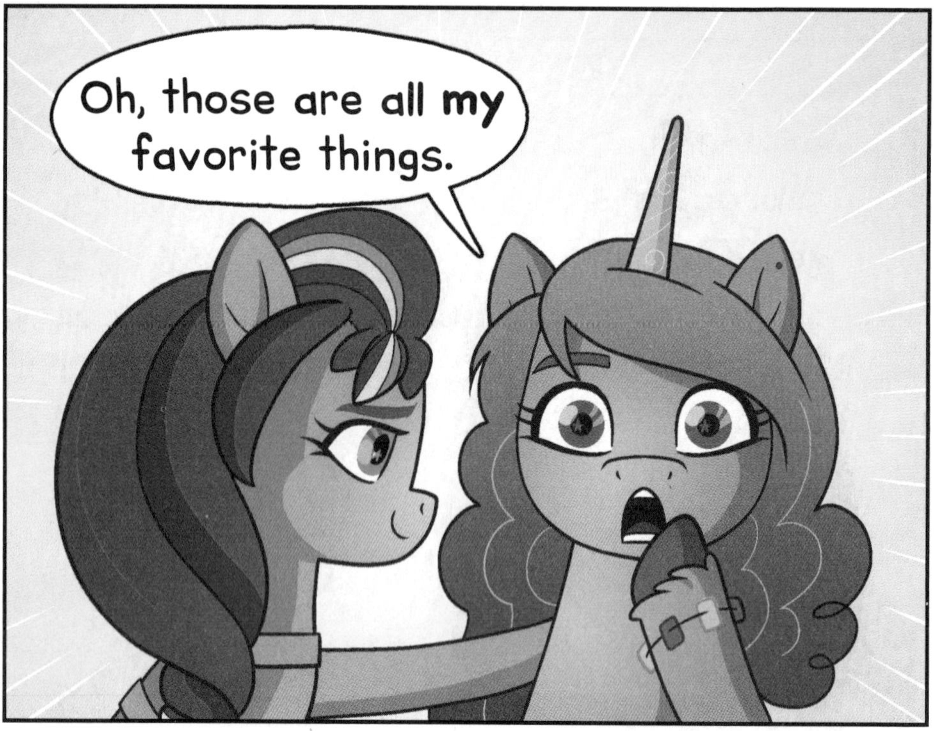
Oh, those are all **my** favorite things.

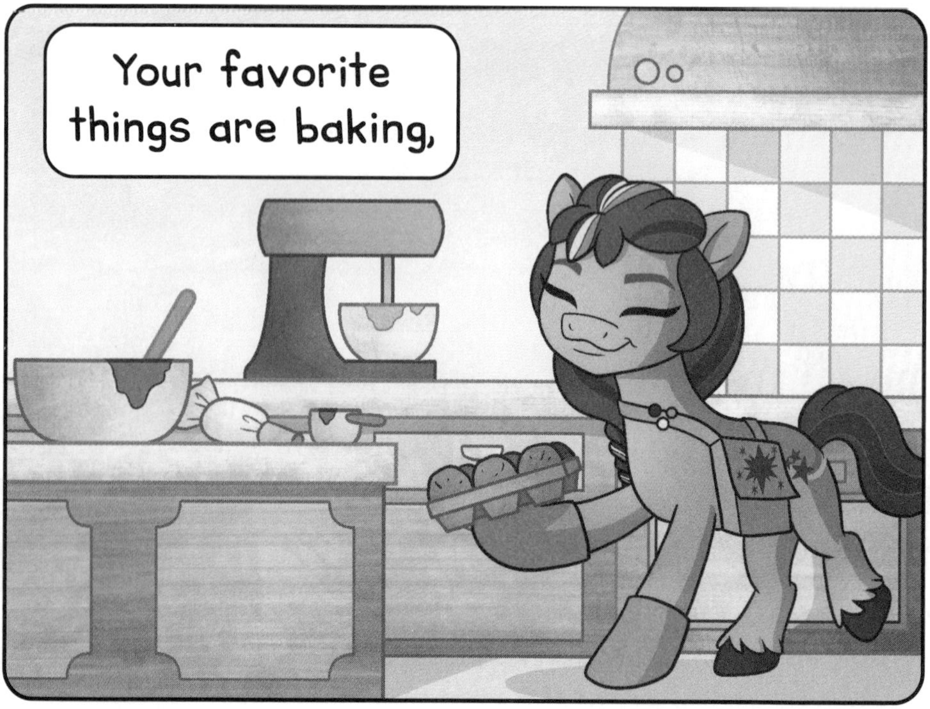
Your favorite things are baking,

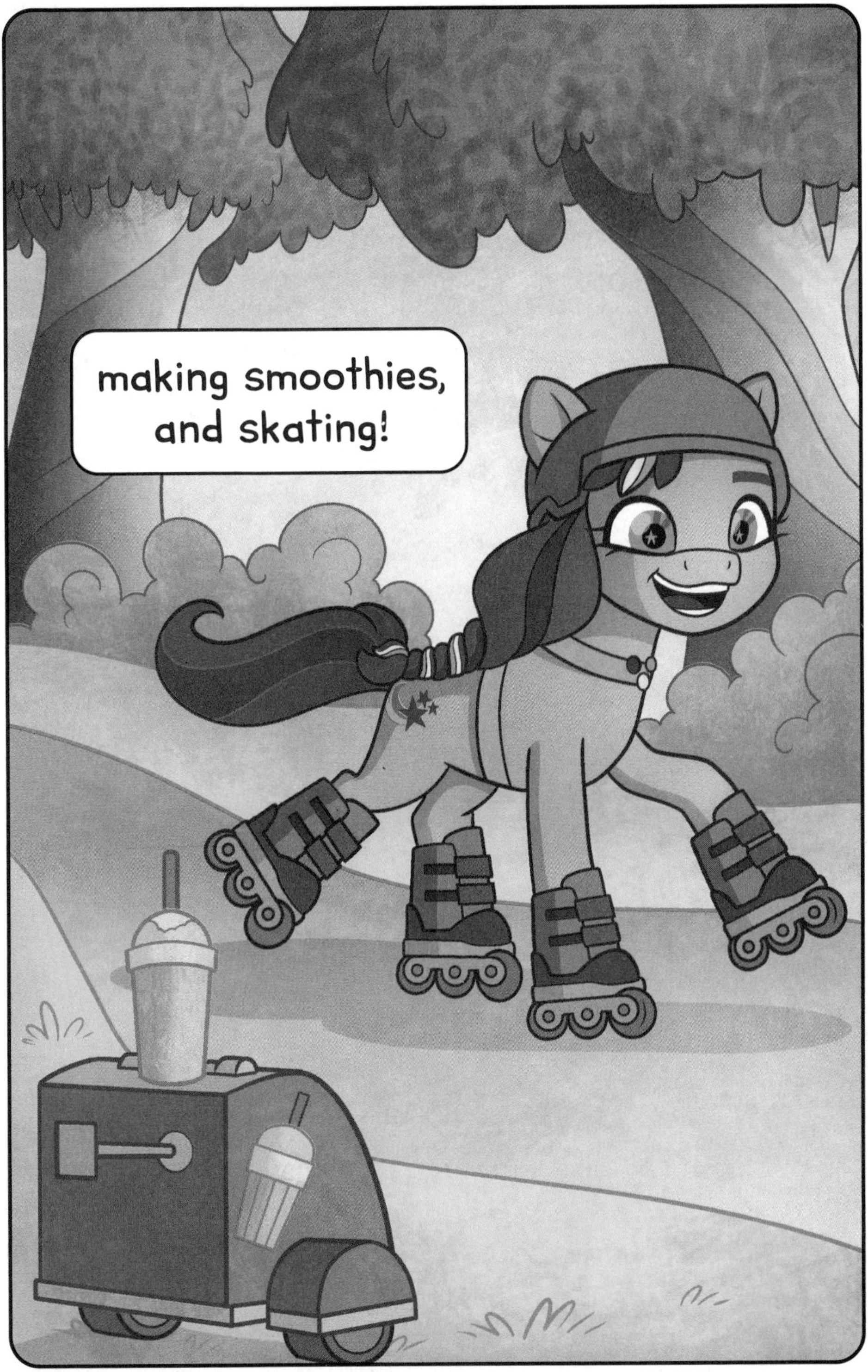
making smoothies,
and skating!

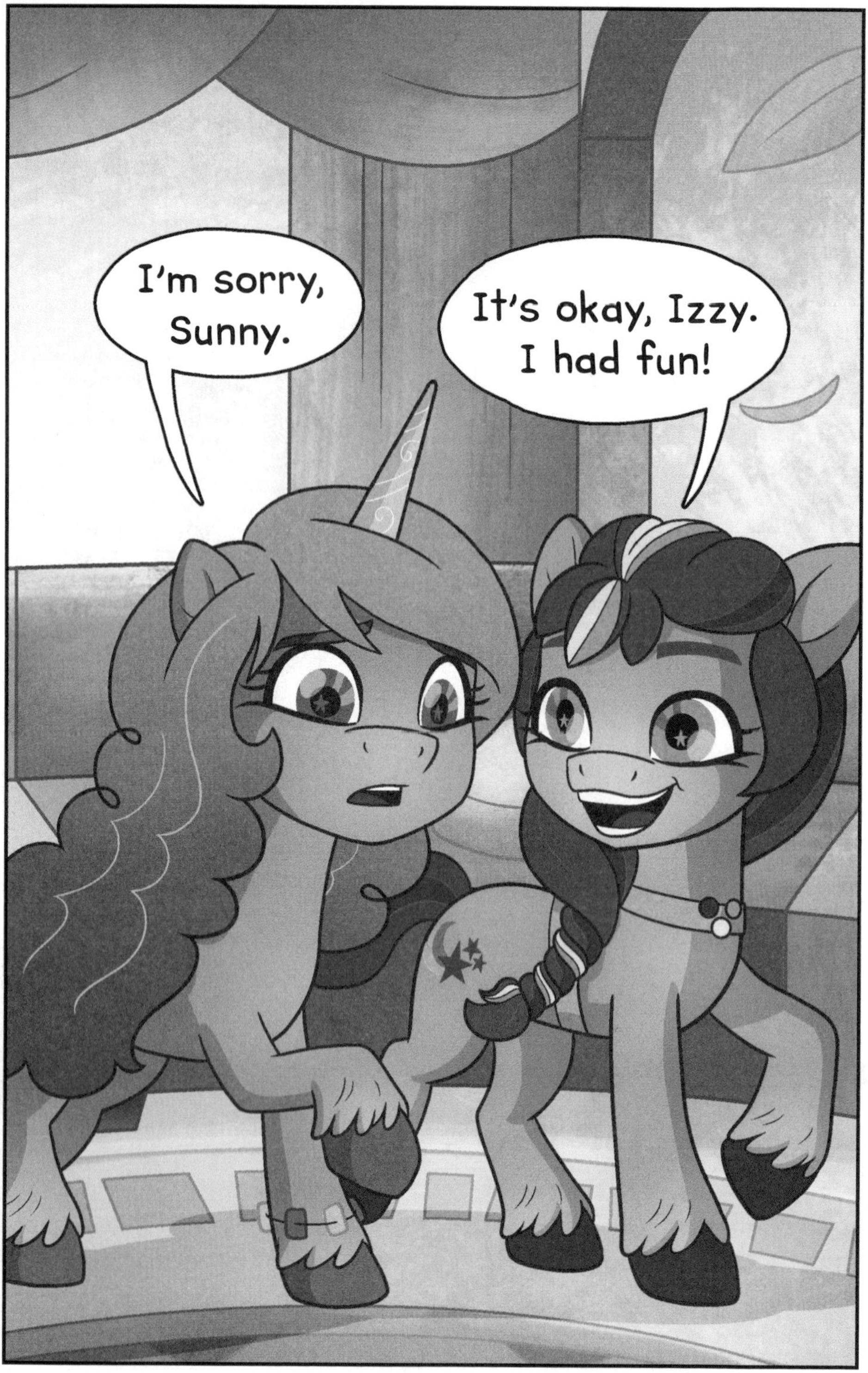
I'm sorry, Sunny.
It's okay, Izzy. I had fun!

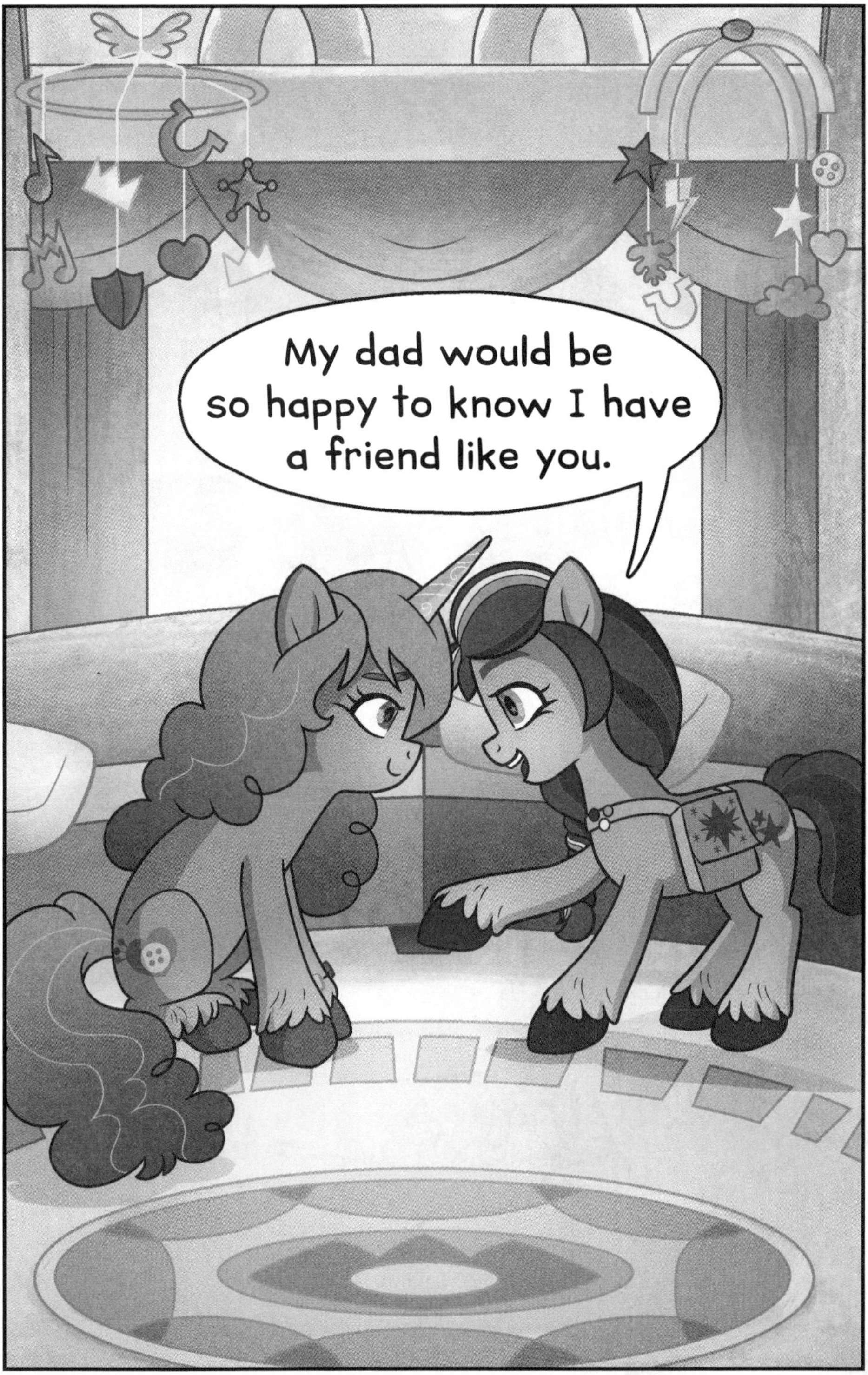
My dad would be so happy to know I have a friend like you.

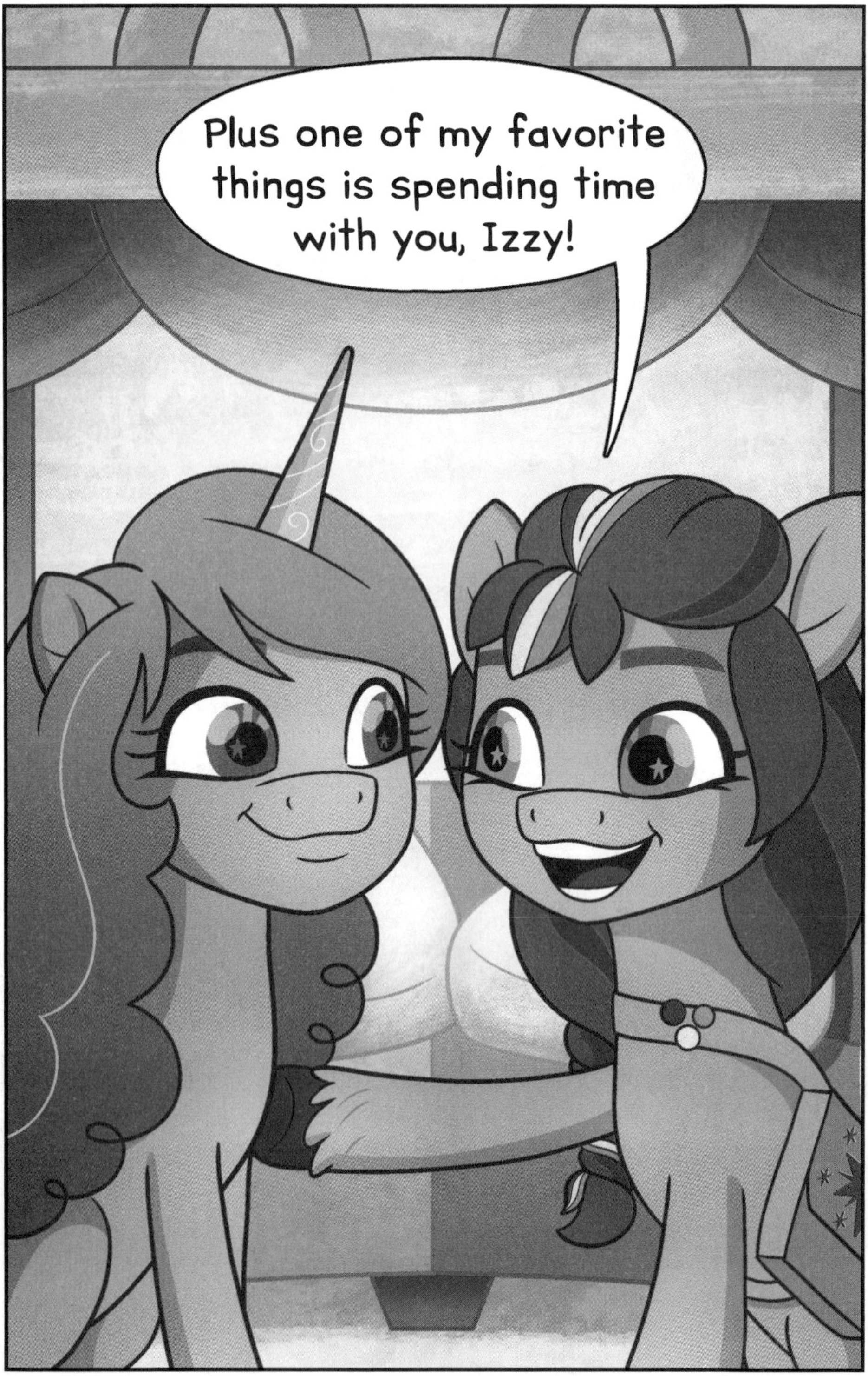
Plus one of my favorite things is spending time with you, Izzy!

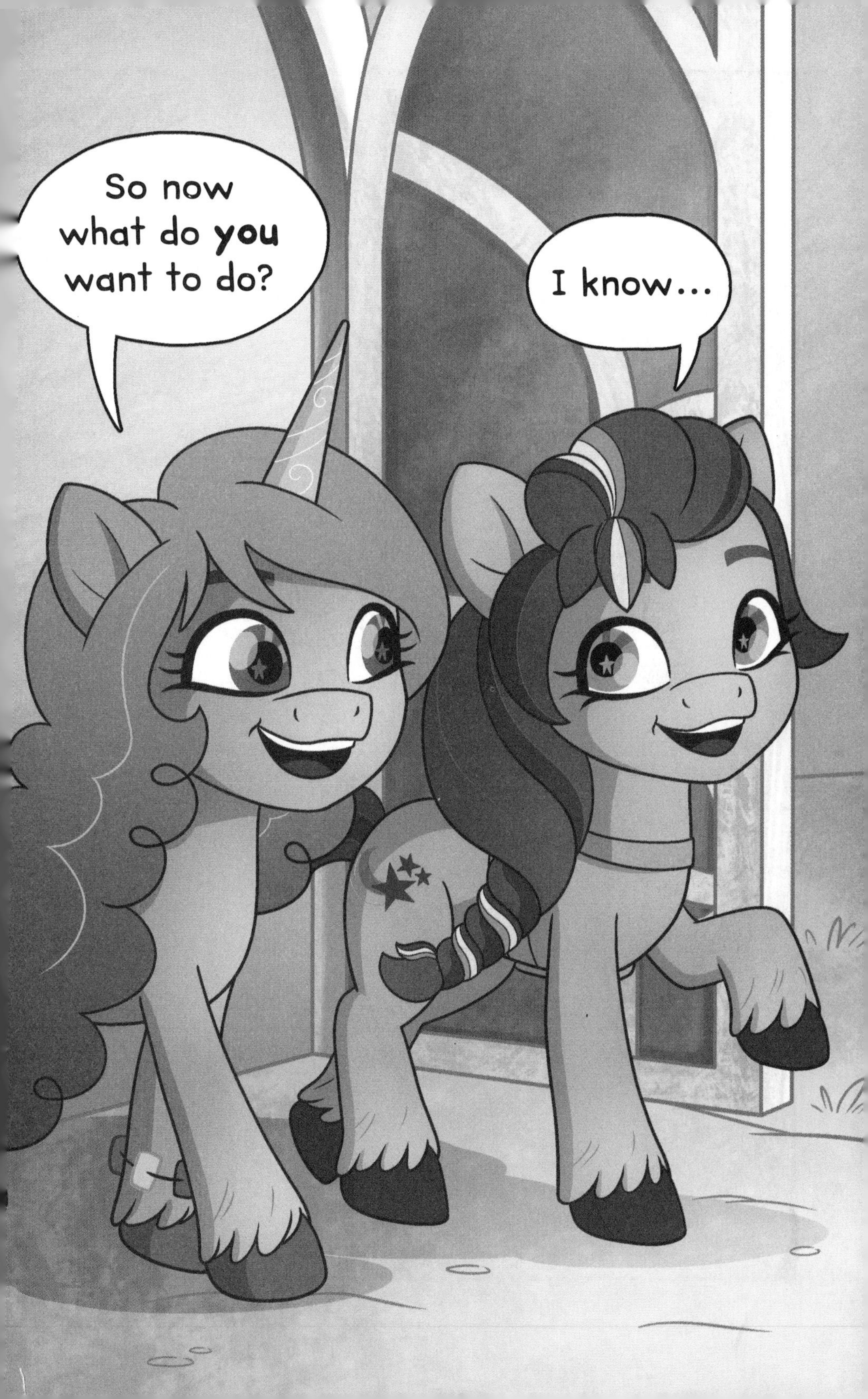
So now what do **you** want to do?
I know...

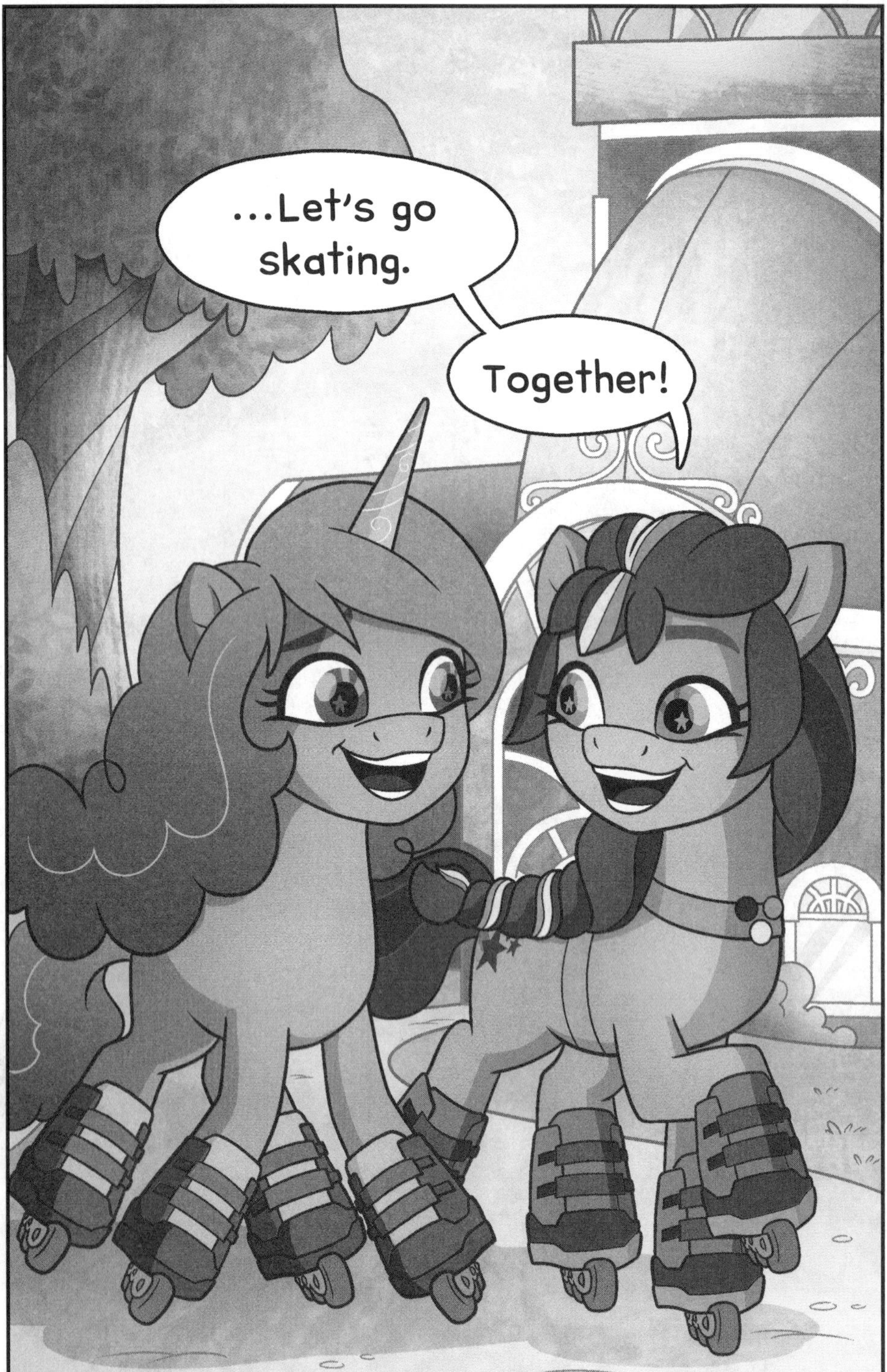
...Let's go skating.
Together!